P9-CIU-426

"No!" Jake shouted, and took off across the room.

One step and Tatiana had the gun in her hands.

The second step and she was training it on Gaia.

The third step and he swore he heard the catch of the trigger.

He threw himself into the air, his eyes locked on Gaia's shocked face. The sound of the gunshot exploded in his ears, and then everything went black.

Don't miss any books in this thrilling series:

FEARLESS™

Available from SIMON PULSE

For orders other than by individual consumers, Simon & Schuster grants a discount on the purchase of **10 or more** copies of single titles for special markets or premium use. For further details, please write to the Vice-President of Special Markets, Pocket Books, 1260 Avenue of the Americas, New York, NY 10020–1586, 8th Floor.

For information on how individual consumers can place orders, please write to Mail Order Department, Simon & Schuster Inc., 100 Front Street, Riverside, NJ 08075.

FEARLESS™

CHASE

FRANCINE PASCAL

J PB F PAS
Pascal, Francine.
Chase /
AMAR   30800002307970

SIMON PULSE
New York   London   Toronto   Sydney   Singapore

If you purchased this book without a cover, you should be aware that this book is stolen property. It was reported as "unsold and destroyed" to the publisher and neither the author nor the publisher has received any payment for this "stripped book."

This book is a work of fiction. Any references to historical events, real people, or real locales are used fictitiously. Other names, characters, places, and incidents are the product of the author's imagination, and any resemblance to actual events or locales or persons, living or dead, is entirely coincidental.

First Simon Pulse edition July 2003

Copyright © 2003 by Francine Pascal

Cover copyright © 2003 by 17th Street Productions, an Alloy company.

SIMON PULSE
An imprint of Simon & Schuster Children's Publishing Division
1230 Avenue of the Americas, New York, NY 10020

Produced by 17th Street Productions, an Alloy company
151 West 26th Street
New York, NY 10001

All rights reserved, including the right of reproduction in whole or in part in any form.
For information address 17th Street Productions, 151 West 26th Street, New York, NY 10001.

Fearless™ is a trademark of Francine Pascal.

Printed in the United States of America
10 9 8 7 6 5 4 3 2 1

Library of Congress Control Number 2003101744
ISBN: 0-689-85765-9

To Nall

When I was very little—I mean braids and teddy bears little—my mother used to read to me from *Little Women* every night before bed. She used to read to me from a lot of books, but *Little Women* is the one I remember the best. Like everyone else who's ever read the book, I wanted to be Jo. Jo was cool. Jo was a writer, even though women weren't supposed to be writers. Jo spurned men. Jo took care of everybody. And above all, Jo wasn't pretty—she was awkward and unkempt and a tomboy. In short, I probably wanted to be Jo because I already *was* Jo. I was never going to be the beautiful, admired, gracious Meg or the sweet, meek, victim Beth. And Amy? I pretty much just wanted to kick that annoying little twit in the head.

But the one thing Jo had that I wanted most was her sisters. (Except Amy.) She would have done anything for them and they for her. There was this bond between

them that was like nothing I had
in my life. My parents were great,
but it wasn't the same. I wanted a
confidant, someone to have adventures with, someone to share my
daydreams and my nightmares with.
Someone who would understand. I
wanted that unconditional love and
friendship that was all over the
pages of *Little Women*.

But as many times as I asked
and begged for a little sister,
the answer was always the same.
"Maybe someday. . . ," my mother
would say, a sad, wistful look in
her eyes. I know she wanted more
kids, but I also know that she
and my father had a seriously
complicated life, what with Loki
sneaking around and pretending he
was my father so he could take me
out of school and coach me and
try to brainwash me. They probably wanted to wait until things
calmed down. Well, they never
did. And then she was killed.

So the closest I ever came to a
sister was Tatiana. I'm not saying
we ever approached anything like

unconditional love, but I would
say we had an understanding. We
lived together, we shared a room,
and our parents were clearly in
love (or so I thought). It was
impossible not to draw the conclu-
sion that we might be sisters one
day and that in some ways we
already were.

You see, we were in it
together. (Again, so I thought.)
We bonded over our superspy parents and the constant level of
mind-bending insanity in our
lives. I thought we were on the
same side—that we would be there
for each other no matter what. And
I could almost see a future where
we'd become really close. It felt
like it was almost destined, you
know? I mean, where else was I
going to find someone who had as
screwed up a life as I did?
Someone who understood it all.

But as usual, I was wrong.
Tatiana betrayed me in a way I never
would have thought possible. She
tried to kill me. Betrayal doesn't
get much more serious than that.

So much for sisters.

Maybe it's true, what they say. Blood *is* thicker than water. You shouldn't trust anyone but your family. Your true family. Your blood.

Huh.

The only blood relative I have that I *know* is alive is Loki. The evil, psychotic, scum-sucking maggot monster of death.

Sometimes the irony of life just makes the head spin.

She couldn't
remember the
last time
she hadn't
gotten worked
unstimulating
up and
focused and
generally
jazzed during
a fight.

IT WASN'T A UNIQUE EXPERIENCE FOR

Gaia Moore, wandering the streets of
New York City with nowhere to go. It
wasn't even a unique experience for
her to believe her father was dead,

Broken

that she was next, that around every corner she passed
could be the gun that held the bullet that
would end her life. It was just that it had been
so long since she had been so entirely alone. Weeks,
even. Months.

There was no one left.

Gaia pulled her collar up against the cold breeze
that blew harder and more bitingly with each passing
moment. It was late spring already, but then,
Manhattan never seemed to adhere to the *Farmer's
Almanac*. The island had taken on the general attitude
of its inhabitants and had mastered the ability to give
an "Up yours!" to even the likes of Mother Nature.
And so here was this winter wind on the heels of a
warm spring day. At least it kept the throngs of people
off the streets and inside, watching their rented
movies and eating their delivery food. Fewer inno-
cents for Gaia to trample. She turned a corner and
bent into the wind.

Just above the soft worn cotton of her jacket, Gaia
made sure her eyes were free and peeled. Natasha had
been captured and was now in the custody of the
CIA. At this very moment she was being questioned,

interrogated, maybe even beaten (one could dream). But Tatiana was still out there somewhere. She could be anywhere. And she still had orders to kill Gaia.

Not if I kill you first, Gaia thought, her rage bubbling over from her heart into her thoughts. It was still hard to swallow, the fact that Tatiana was in on it. The fact that everything they'd been through together had been a lie. That she'd actually been snowed by a little blond DKNY-sporting fake. In the beginning Tatiana had acted so helpless, like she didn't know how to fight, like she didn't understand the simple art of tracking someone. How many times had Gaia risked her own neck to help Tatiana? And she'd actually been proud of the way Tatiana was coming along. How she was learning to take care of herself, kick some butt of her own. Even if she was also turning into a materialistic, party-animal Friend of Heather. But it was all an act.

"It doesn't matter," Gaia spoke into the collar of her jacket, her warm breath heating her cheeks and mouth. So she'd lost Tatiana. Big deal. She'd lost more important people in her lifetime. Much more important. And if she bumped into the girl right now, she'd kick the crap out of her first and ask questions later. One question, actually. The only one that mattered.

Where is my father?

Yes, Natasha had claimed that he was dead. And Gaia had no reason not to believe her. Except, of course, that everything else the woman had ever said or done had been a lie. At this point Gaia gave her father a fifty-fifty chance of still being down with the breathing folk. But she was a hundred percent sure that Tatiana knew the truth. And those were good odds to be working with.

`If she only knew where the hell the girl was.`

"All alone, no place to go, all alone, no place to go."

Gaia paused for a moment, taken off guard by the rambling words of the homeless man who suddenly blocked her path. He looked at her with wild, blank eyes, shaking a battered blue-and-white coffee cup in front of her, the piddling change inside rattling pathetically. He was bundled inside about four flannel coats but somehow still looked impossibly cold. He shuffled toward her, his gooey gaze settling somewhere around the bridge of her nose.

"All alone, no place to go, all alone, no place to go. . ."

She knew he was just one of the thousands of unlucky people who had been driven insane by a life on the streets, but for a moment it felt like he was looking right through her skin into her heart. Somehow he was extracting the exact words she was trying to keep from eating away at her.

"All alone, no place to go, all alone, no place to go. . ."

"All right, all right!" Gaia said. She stuffed her hand into the depths of her jeans pocket and came out with a quarter. "Here," she said, slapping the coin into the cup. The man didn't acknowledge it—he simply took up the refrain once more.

"All alone, no place to go, all alone, no place to go. . ."

Gaia started to run.

She ran to feel the wind on her face, to get her blood pumping, to hear the roar of the cars and people passing by in her ears, to drown out the man's ceaseless words.

"All alone, no place to go, all alone, no place to go. . ."

She ran and ran, without even realizing that she was headed for Ed's building until she was standing right in front of it. The tears that had been ripped from her eyes by the stinging wind made little streaks across her temples, tightening the skin. Gaia pulled in a breath and hugged her jacket to herself. She stared at the door.

This was it. This was the place she always used to be able to come to when there was no place else to go. Ed had been the one person who was there for her, without fail. But she'd screwed that up, too, hadn't she? She'd screwed everything up.

Trying not to think about the comfort that lay just beyond those sleek glass doors, Gaia turned her steps toward Washington Square Park. It was time to admit the inevitable. If she was going to get any rest tonight, which she'd need if she was going to track down Tatiana tomorrow, then she was going to have to scare herself up a park bench. Washington Square Park was downtown's Motel 6 for runaways and druggies. The only difference was a person didn't need to lay out any cash to get a bed.

Gaia slipped into the park by the west entrance and started along the circle. A large woman dozed, sitting up, on the first bench, surrounded by dozens of shopping bags full of clothing and rags and heaven only knew what else. There was a shopping cart tied to the bench by a red bandanna, and a kitten was curled up in the child's seat among a bunch of tangled scarves. On the next bench was a scrawny kid wearing barely enough clothing to keep him comfortable on a hot summer's day, shivering away even as he slept. Gaia averted her eyes and swallowed back her pity. He was probably an addict who had left a perfectly good home behind him somewhere, and at that moment Gaia couldn't feel sorry for him. All she could think about was the warm bed out there with his name on it.

Finally Gaia came across an empty bench, and she glanced around to make sure the immediate area was creep-free. Satisfied, she lay down, her face toward the back of the seat, and curled her arm under her head.

Don't think about anything, she told herself. *You can deal with it all tomorrow.*

Soon Gaia felt herself starting to drift, and she silently thanked the stars for her ability to fall asleep anywhere. But just as her thoughts were fading to black, the entire bench shook from the force of a powerful blow. Gaia sat up straight and looked right into the stubble-covered face of a square-shouldered, square-jawed, totally strung-out junkie. His eyes were lined with red and his breathing was ragged. He bared his teeth like a rabid dog.

"This is my bench, girlie," he said, gracing Gaia with a cloud of breath that smelled of rotten beer.

"Leave me alone," Gaia said, starting to lie down again. She was definitely not in the mood.

The junkie walked around to the front of the bench, grabbed the back of Gaia's jacket, and yanked her to the ground. Her shoulder hit the asphalt and her head bounced against the hard ground. Quickly Gaia rolled over onto her back, grimacing. She scrunched up her nose and tried not to breathe.

"Look, when I got here, the bench was empty," Gaia said. "You don't look like the brightest guy in the world, but I'm sure you've heard of finders keepers."

"F'you won't give up the bench, I got no problem takin' it from ya," the guy said.

Gaia rolled her eyes. For once, she didn't feel like fighting, but she'd already had more than enough of the grandstanding banter part of the evening. She had a feeling that this was the type of guy who could stand here and trade threats until he passed out, but there was no telling how long that would take. Besides, the sweet taste of sleep was still clinging to her, and she wanted to get back there. So she decided to take the shortcut. She reached out and shoved him.

The junkie staggered back, surprised, then narrowed his eyes and threw a wide, arcing punch. Gaia easily blocked it, grasped his arm, and turned into him, jabbing her elbow back into his stomach. He doubled over slightly, and she brought her skull back into his with a crack. When she spun away from him and took her fighting stance, he already looked pretty beaten up. Gaia was about to let down her guard when he let out a battle cry and rushed her, tackling her right to the ground.

Gaia tried to push him off her, waiting for her adrenaline to kick in, waiting for that rush of energy, but it didn't come. She was just tired. And not a little bit bored. As she contemplated this, the junkie got one good punch into her gut and another to her jaw that sent stars across her vision. Gaia had had enough. She propped her calves under his torso and lifted, flipping him up and over her head onto his back. He let out a groan as he fell, and Gaia got to her feet to hover over him.

"Are we done yet?" she asked.

He waved his hands in front of his face and winced. "We're done! We're done! Please don't hurt me!"

"Fine," Gaia said, trying not to show how relieved she was. "Just get the hell out of here."

The junkie stood up, keeping his distance from Gaia, then ran off awkwardly into the night. Gaia trudged back over to her bench, feeling heavy and low and disappointed. She couldn't remember the last time she hadn't gotten worked up and focused and generally jazzed during a fight. And right now she felt about as alive as she did in her highly unstimulating math class every day. What was wrong with her? It wasn't like she hadn't been in places as depressing as this before. She'd spent almost her entire life in them.

But this time was somehow different. When she reached inside and tried to summon up some kind of motivating emotion—anger, vengefulness—all she felt was...broken.

Gaia lay down on the bench again, her brow furrowed as she put her head down on the pillow of her bent arm.

Don't think about anything, she told herself again. *You can deal with it all tomorrow.*

Then she closed her eyes and let sleep finally come.

Safe House

TATIANA'S HAND SHOOK VIOLENTLY as she attempted for the third time to master the simple act of inserting a key into a lock. She blamed her shivering on the fact that she hadn't expected the sudden shift in the weather and so hadn't dressed for it. She also hadn't expected, however, to see her mother get dragged off by a couple of huge men in black spy gear.

"Damn it. You must focus," she said to herself through her teeth. If her mother could see her now, she'd be ashamed. Tatiana had to pull herself together. Her mother was counting on her.

Finally Tatiana gripped her right hand with her left to steady it, and mercifully the key slid into the lock. There was a moment of suspense as she turned it, but the lock clicked and the door swung open with a slow, `angry creak,` as if it had just been woken from a deep slumber. Tatiana had the right place. She was home.

She slipped through the door and quickly punched the code her mother had made her memorize into the keypad on the near wall, the red light flashing menacingly as she worked. After hitting all the numbers, Tatiana pressed her thumb into the enter key and squeezed her eyes shut. The alarm let out a loud beep, and when she opened her eyes again, the red light had turned to green. Tatiana closed the door behind her and fastened all five safety locks. She leaned back against the door and allowed herself to breathe. She was safe. Alone, but safe.

Peeling off her lightweight jacket, Tatiana decided

to explore her new abode. In the semidarkness she found a light switch and flicked it on, illuminating the small living room with the weak light from a single overhead fixture. She'd been hearing about the Alphabet City safe house ever since she and her mother had arrived in New York City, but she'd never been here. The moment she saw the place in the light, she felt an almost painful longing for the lofty space of the Seventy-second Street apartment.

Your mother is most likely in a jail cell right now, she told herself. *Quit your whining.*

She breathed in the musty, sooty smell of the air and took a few steps into the tiny square living room. The walls were plain and white, and an old but comfortable-looking corduroy couch stood to one side. A table next to it held a single glass lamp with a dingy shade. Tatiana walked over to the one piece of artwork on the wall—a framed print of Renoir's *The Luncheon of the Boating Party*—and lifted it from the nail that held it in place. Just as she'd been told, there was a square, gray safe door built into the wall. Tatiana quickly dialed in the combination, which she'd also committed to memory, and the door popped open, letting out a hiss of air.

There were stacks upon stacks of bills inside— American dollars, Canadian dollars, Mexican pesos, British pounds, and Russian rubles. Tatiana grabbed a few twenties from one of the bundles of dollars, then pulled out a stack of passports. As she flipped through them—there were at least ten with her picture, each from a different country—she smirked sadly at the names her mother had given her. Annie Whitmore, Corrine Deveneaux, Marianna Alonso, Marcella Tuscano.

I could just disappear, Tatiana thought, allowing the seduction of such a thought to momentarily send her pulse racing. She gazed at her picture on the Italian passport and imagined it—imagined herself on the white sands of the Mediterranean, sipping something fruity and letting her bare back bathe in the sun. But as quickly as the image came, she squelched it. She wasn't going anywhere without her mother. Not now. Not ever.

She took the last items out of the safe, a nice, sleek .45 pistol and a full clip, then crammed the passports back inside. She shoved the clip into the gun, savoring the menacing click as it locked into place. After making sure the safety was on, Tatiana slipped the gun between her waistband and her back. Then she closed the safe and hung the painting again. She had to check the rest of her provisions.

The kitchen, just to the left of the living room, which was lined with avocado green cabinets and held a large brown refrigerator, clearly hadn't been redecorated since the seventies. Tatiana walked over to the pantry and checked inside. The shelves were stocked with canned soups, pasta sauces, packets of instant oatmeal, and cans of soda and juice.

She walked back across the living room to the bedroom, which took all of three steps, and flicked on the light. Two twin-size beds, draped with blue blankets, stood on either side of a single nightstand. Inspection of a small dresser against the far wall revealed drawers filled with plain underwear, bras, T-shirts, and sweaters in Tatiana and Natasha's sizes. The closet held a few pairs of jeans, assorted footwear, and two heavy winter coats. On the top shelf was a wide array of wigs, hats, and sunglasses. Tatiana pulled down a long, dark wig with natural-looking waves and smiled morosely. Her mother had certainly been prepared.

Still fingering the coarse hair of the wig, Tatiana sat down on the closest bed and tried to remain calm. She tried not to let herself picture the events of the evening over and over again. Reliving the nightmare was not going to help her deal with it. It wasn't going to bring her mother back to her. There was only one thing that would. She had to make Gaia talk. Gaia was the only person who knew where her mother was—who the men were that had taken her.

From their uniform fighting tactics, it was clear they belonged to some government agency, and considering Tom Moore's affiliation with the CIA, Tatiana assumed it was them. But that meant nothing to her. It wasn't as if she was privy to all the CIA's secret interrogation facilities. As much as she hated to admit it, she needed Gaia. Unfortunately, she knew that the self-righteous, egotistical bitch-on-a-mission was never going to help her.

What Tatiana needed was a plan.

Taking a deep breath, Tatiana gathered her blond hair on top of her head and pulled the wig on over it. It was tight, but all the better. She tugged at the temples, then walked over to the full-length mirror that was attached to the back of the door, suddenly hyper-aware of the cold steel against the skin of her back. When she saw her reflection, she smiled slowly. It was perfect—a total transformation.

Tatiana pulled her gun out of her waistband, hoisted it, and aimed it at her reflection, her arms straight and locked at the elbow. She barely even recognized herself. Whatever her plan might turn out to be, Gaia would never see her coming.

GAIA KEPT HER HEAD BENT, EYES

focused on the grimy sidewalk as she emerged from the subway station on East Sixty-eighth Street. It was rush hour, and she was **So Blind** bombarded on every side by harried commuters, juggling their coffee cups and briefcases and reeking of musky aftershave and freshly sprayed perfume. Gaia's intention had been to remain inconspicuous, but among this crowd there was no way to keep from sticking out like a prune in a bushel of apples. She stepped to the corner and looked left and right, trying to pick out anything suspicious. Any signs of Tatiana.

The three guys who always hung out by the tiny newsstand across Lexington were there as usual, checking out the latest issue of *Boobs* magazine and sneering as they hovered over the centerfold. Mr. Han, the Vietnamese grocer, stood outside his shop, guarding his fruit with a watchful eye. A bus zoomed by, kicking a cloud of exhaust directly into Gaia's lungs. Yep. Everything was status normal.

The light changed and Gaia crossed the street, fully aware that she was taking her life in her own hands simply by appearing in this neighborhood. It was the one thing, besides school, that she and Tatiana had in common. The girl would have to be an idiot not to look for Gaia here. If Tatiana knew anything about her mark, she had to know that Gaia would come back to the apartment to look for clues. And as a morning breeze tossed a tangled clump of hair across Gaia's vision, she almost hoped she *would* bump into Tatiana. It would be nice to get this over with.

When she arrived at her building, Gaia nodded quickly at Javier, the doorman, then hopped into an open elevator. As she slowly made her ascent, she wondered exactly how long it would take the CIA to break Natasha. They were probably using all the standard tactics—sleep deprivation, starvation, threats against her daughter—to try to get her to talk. But Natasha was trained by some of the best in the world. She could cope with torture. Gaia knew it could take days, weeks, months before the government was able to get the information Gaia needed. She didn't have that long.

The elevator pinged and the doors slid open. Gaia cautiously peeked into the hallway and found it deserted. She crept along the wall to the apartment she had been sharing with Natasha and Tatiana for so many weeks. Pressing her ear up against the door's flat surface, she heard nothing but merciful silence. Gaia slid her key into the lock and opened the door.

The moment she stepped inside, she knew instinctively that the place was deserted. It felt cold and still, almost as if no one had inhabited its rooms for years. As she stood and looked around at the living room she'd kicked back in and the kitchen she'd snacked from, Gaia was filled with a hot, suffocating shame. How could she have let Natasha and Tatiana fool her into thinking they cared? How could she have been so blind?

She thought of all the times Natasha had scolded her for being late, of the concern she'd shown for her and her father. But suddenly she saw the bigger picture. Natasha had laughed at her in these rooms. She'd manipulated her and had enjoyed doing it. Poor little Gaia. Poor little naive daughter of Tom. And all the while Tatiana had been in on it. Tatiana had been laughing at her, too.

Gaia hated that she'd allowed it to happen. She hated that she had been so gullible. But not anymore. She was in control now. Now it was her turn to laugh. Gaia locked the door behind her and set to work.

And just as she had done earlier, when she'd been looking for clues to the attempts made on her life, she turned the apartment inside out. She started with Natasha's room, ripping through the clothes in the closet and checking every nook and cranny for hidden compartments, false walls. She knocked along the surfaces, searching for hollow spaces, but there was nothing. The shelves were stacked with shoe boxes and bags. Gaia pulled every one down and emptied them on the floor in a pile, but the search revealed nothing except the fact that Natasha was clearly obsessed with her feet.

Frustrated, Gaia checked under the bed, pulling out every single drawer and overturning them, emptying silky nightgowns, cashmere sweaters, and slippery scarves onto the bed. She could vividly see Natasha in this room, getting dressed, smirking her triumph in the full-length mirror, thinking of how easily she'd seduced Tom Moore. Gaia felt hot tears spring to her eyes. This was the first woman her father had trusted

21

since her mother had died. How was it that her father, who had been a spy for over twenty years, was so damned gullible? How could he have let her mother's memory be marred by someone like Natasha?

A sliver of anger worked its way into Gaia's heart, but she wiped her tears and tried to suppress it. This was not her father's fault. There was no use wasting time wishing things were different. Wishing he hadn't let his guard down. Gaia herself had mistakenly trusted many an enemy.

She dropped the last empty drawer on the bed, then checked under each one for documents that might be taped there and inspected lamps and phones, looking for wires. By the time she was done, the bedroom was chaos, the bathroom a total wreck of smashed eye shadows and broken bottles.

But there was nothing. If Natasha had been hiding anything in this room, she was damn good.

Gaia rushed into the hall and paused for a moment, listening for any sign of life, but didn't hear a sound. She attacked the room she shared with Tatiana with the same ferocity, ripping her precious clothes from the hangers and pawing through her schoolbooks. She yanked bags and boxes out from under Tatiana's bed and emptied her CD collection onto the floor. But again there was nothing.

Gaia sighed and pressed her palm into her forehead. Maybe this was pointless. Maybe she was just wasting her time. Her blood rushed through her veins as a little voice in her mind taunted her for being so stupid. Natasha wasn't an amateur. She wouldn't keep the secrets of her master plan right under the nose of one of her primary targets.

Still, Gaia wasn't quite ready to give up. Her father was depending on her. Alive or dead, she had to find out where he was, and as far as Gaia knew, Natasha and Tatiana were the only ones who had that information. She hit Natasha's room again, and the moment she walked in, she realized she hadn't checked the nightstands. She dropped to her knees in front of the closest one and yanked the small drawer out. It flew open and then stuck stubbornly. As much as Gaia jimmied and tugged, the drawer wouldn't come free. Gaia pulled out the paperback novel, the pad of paper and pen, and the sleep mask inside, dropping it all to the floor at her knees. She shoved her hands into the empty drawer and felt along the plywood surface.

"Come on," Gaia said under her breath, starting to feel desperate. A trickle of sweat ran down from her temple along her cheek. "Come on. . . ."

And then her fingertip hit something. Something sharp. Gaia's heart leapt into her throat. She ran her fingertip along the slim edge of what had to be a small envelope, from the feel of it. She pulled out her hands and crouched, tilting her head to one side and trying to see into the back of the drawer. Sure enough, she spotted the folded edge of a brown envelope that was wedged into the seam between the back of the drawer and the bottom. Gaia reached into the drawer again, grasped the envelope with both hands, and yanked as hard as she could.

The envelope came free and Gaia tumbled backward into the pile of shoes and boots behind her. Her heart slammed against her rib cage in excitement as she looked at the envelope. Across the front five capital letters were printed: *ABCSH*.

There was something heavy inside. Gaia tipped the envelope over her hand, and into her waiting palm fell a single brass key. It lay there, cold and unhelpful, but Gaia felt like she'd achieved a small victory. It was a clue. It had to be. The key had been just hidden enough and the message on the front of the envelope was just cryptic enough to reassure her that she was on to something.

Gaia slipped the key back into the envelope and stuffed it into her back pocket. She returned to her room, grabbed her duffel bag from under her bed, and stuffed some clothes into it at random. She slung her messenger bag over her shoulder, took one last look around at the destruction she'd caused, and headed for the door.

She had no idea where she was going, but she couldn't stay here. Aside from the possibility of being murdered by Tatiana in her sleep, this place had too many bad memories. Memories of how for weeks on end, she'd been sleeping with the enemy.

It was time to start over. Something Gaia was growing more and more accustomed to.

ABCSH, ABCSH, A. . . B. . . C. . . S. . . H.

Another Enemy

Gaia stared at the corner of the chessboard, the squares and playing pieces blurred before her. She'd come to the park hoping that a nice solid trouncing of Mr. Haq would help calm her nerves, help her focus, but all she could think about was the letters. They danced in front of her mind's eye like one of those animated lessons from *Sesame Street,* but they refused to form themselves into any kind of order that would yield an answer.

ABCSH. . .

What did it mean? And what did it have to do with her father?

"Girlie?" Mr. Haq said. "Girlie? Your move!" He snapped his stubby, calloused fingers in front of Gaia's dazed face.

She blinked, and her eyes settled on the board.

"I got you this time, eh, girlie?" the old man said gleefully, rubbing his palms together. "You not yourself today. I on top of my game." He snickered and Gaia sighed. She could take him in five moves, no problem, but she couldn't see the point. This was totally useless. The game had done nothing to calm her down. She had to get out of here. She had to go. . . somewhere, she just didn't know where. All she knew was that she felt like she had millions of tiny little Ping-Pong balls dancing around under her skin. She couldn't just sit here any longer.

"I have to go," she said, standing up.

Mr. Haq's tiny, dark eyes widened as he tilted back his head to look up at her. "You forfeit? You can't forfeit! You never forfeit!"

"First time for everything," Gaia said flatly.

"But I have you! I have you!" Mr. Haq wailed in protest, gesturing wildly at the board. "You can't just leave because I have you!"

"Sorry," Gaia said. She shouldered her messenger bag, grabbed her duffel, and hurried away, followed by the continued sounds of Mr. Haq's protesting wails.

Gaia crossed over to Waverly and started to walk east with less than no clue as to where she was headed. She immediately regretted forfeiting her game. At least as long as she was sitting there, she was *somewhere*.

Somewhere familiar. Now she was headed right back to nowhere.

If only she knew what her next move should be. If only she had some idea of where Tatiana was. But by now she could be in another state. She could be in another country. Gaia had waited too long. With each passing moment Tatiana gained an advantage. She was slowly slipping through Gaia's fingers.

Gaia continued to wander, letting the Walk and Don't Walk signs define her path. When she hit the corner of Second Street and Second Avenue, she heard the sharp start of a scream that was quickly cut short. Gaia's senses went on the alert as she looked around, searching for something amiss, wondering if she'd just imagined it. But then something caught her eye. A few figures struggling right in the center of the ages-old cemetery across the street.

Gaia dashed into traffic, ignoring the angry horn of a large meat truck that had to skid to a stop, and tossed her bags over the iron fence that surrounded the cemetery. She scrambled up and over the barrier. As she ran toward the fray, she saw that two average-size men were trying to pull the purse off a middle-aged woman who was struggling on the ground. The strap was wrapped around her body and under her arm, making it difficult for the guys to get it free. But they soon would, and who knew what they would do to the woman once they had what they wanted?

"Hey!" Gaia called out, bending at the waist.

The two men looked up in surprise, and Gaia used the moment to rush straight at the slightly taller guy, shoulder first. He didn't even have a chance to throw out his arms. Gaia hit him hard, and he let out an "Oof!" before tumbling to the ground with her in a mass of tangled limbs. Gaia was just getting her bearings to pummel the crap out of him when his buddy came up behind her and got her in a headlock. He yanked her away from his friend, and Gaia felt her eyes bulge as her windpipe was cut off. She choked and sputtered, grasping at the guy's arm with both hands.

"Don't go nowhere," her assailant said to the woman on the ground.

Gaia tried to shoot her a look, telling her to run, but she knew that her widened eyes, probably just made her look panicked. The woman wept and pulled her leg toward her. It was twisted unnaturally and was probably broken. So much for running.

"Yo, Tino, we got a spark plug here," the headlock guy said.

Tino, who had a nice scar that cut from the corner of his eye all the way down to the corner of his mouth, scrambled to his feet and fixed Gaia with a menacing glare. He slowly cracked his knuckles, then came at her, fast. But at the last second Gaia pushed her feet off the ground, used every muscle in her abs to bring up her legs, and double kicked Tino right in his nasty face.

The force of his momentum worked against him, and Tino crumbled to the ground, knocked out. The guy behind Gaia loosened his grip in surprise and she ducked out from under his arm, turned, and landed a nice right hook across his nose. His hands flew up to cover it, and she punched him once in the gut and kicked him in the groin. When he fell to his knees, she finished him off with an elbow jab to the back of his neck.

He hit the ground in a fetal position, unconscious. Gaia looked down at her handiwork—two knocked-out thugs in short order—and waited for a nice sense of satisfaction to come over her, but it didn't. She was still antsy. She was still made up of Ping-Pong balls.

"Are you okay?" Gaia asked the woman, who was now leaning back against a headstone.

She turned amazed eyes on Gaia. "I need to take a self-defense class," she said.

Gaia frowned. "I think your leg is broken. I'm gonna go get some help." The woman eyed her two attackers warily. "Don't worry about them," Gaia assured her. "They're down for the count."

She jogged over to her bags, grabbed them up, and this time found the open gate to exit the cemetery. A block and a half away she spotted a parked patrol car and told the officer behind the wheel that there was a woman hurt back at the graveyard and that the two guys who'd hurt her were still there. He picked up his radio and called it in.

"Don't move," he told Gaia as he turned on his siren. "We'll want your statement."

"Right," Gaia said. And the moment he peeled away, she took off in the other direction.

ABCSH. . . ABCSH, her brain started up again. What was it? What *was* it? She wished she had someone to talk to—someone to bounce this clue off and see what they came up with. Someone to brainstorm with. But there was no one left. Ed hated her. Sam hated her. There was no one else who knew about her psychotic family—her psychotic life. And there was certainly no one she knew who was up on espionage. No code crackers in her immediate acquaintance.

Except, of course. . .

Gaia stopped in her tracks so fast, the woman behind her walked right into her.

"Excuse me!" the lady snapped as she righted her bags and shuffled around Gaia.

But Gaia was in the midst of an epiphany—a bona fide brainstorm. *Loki.* As long as Gaia had lived, every awful thing that had ever happened to her had been perpetrated by Loki. Gaia had always thought it was just a little too weird that her father had fallen into a random coma the same day Loki had become comatose himself.

Gaia stepped out of the foot traffic of the sidewalk,

her mind reeling. What if Loki's men *had* caused her father's coma? What if Loki *was* responsible for her father being kidnapped from the hospital and taken who knew where? That would have to mean that Natasha was working with Loki's men. . . and maybe even Loki himself.

I haven't checked up on him since he was put in the hospital, Gaia thought. *Not once.*

Gaia had never had a chance to find out who Natasha and Tatiana were working for. Were they employed by some unknown agency—some new adversary—or were they just more of Loki's operatives? Was it possible that Loki had woken up and somehow escaped? Was it possible that he was calling the shots once again?

It was a slim chance, but it was the only lead Gaia had. If Loki was out there somewhere, she needed to know. At least she would have some idea of what she was up against. And if he was still safely tucked away in his coma, then she would know for sure that she and her father had another enemy.

With an actual purpose, an actual destination in mind, Gaia finally felt her nerves start to relax. She rolled back her shoulders and headed for the subway.

Gaia is starting to crack. I can tell. She's been wandering the city without purpose all day. The longest she has stayed still was the half hour she spent at our old apartment. I imagine she was tearing it to shreds. It doesn't bother me, however. I know she didn't find anything there. My mother is nothing if not careful.

Since then she has been through Central Park, across Columbus Circle, through Midtown, down Fifth Avenue to Washington Square, where she played a game of chess for five minutes, and then into the East Village, where she found a fight. Of course. For a moment I was concerned that she was headed for the safe house—she came very close to that neighborhood—but then she suddenly stopped. She stared at nothing for a few moments and got on the subway. And all this time she has never looked behind her. She's had a crazed sort of look in her eye all day, and she never even suspected I was following.

Like I said, she's cracking up.

And I could have killed her so many times. So many times I almost pulled out the gun and ended it. It was as if the weapon was calling to me, taunting me, telling me to finish her off. It is, after all, what my mother wants.

But I can't. Not yet. Without Gaia I will never find out where my mother is.

There has to be some way to get to her. Some way to trick her into meeting with me. Someone I can use as a decoy. But as far as I can see, I have only two not very attractive options.

One is Ed, but I will not put him in the middle of this. I could not bear it if he were killed. He is the one mistake I have made in all this time. I was not supposed to care for anyone, but I do care for Ed. Until I met him, I did not believe that any person in this world could be truly good. I didn't believe in friendship or in pure intention. But Ed is different. He is a good person, and he does not deserve to die just because he was stupid enough to fall in love with Gaia and be friends with me. Maybe that is his one flaw. His stupid heart.

But even if a small part of me wanted to be with him, I realize it is better that we were never really together. I would only break his heart like Gaia has so many times. Because once I'm done with Gaia, I'm gone.

Two is Sam. But Sam has no reason to trust me. In fact, he has every reason not to.

So I'm back at the first square. Too bad Gaia is such a friendless loser. It just makes my job harder. I have to think. There has to be *someone*, doesn't there? There just *has* to be. . . .

Was he going
to have to
date FBI
chicks and
cops and, **normal**
like,
girl
vampire
slayers or
something
for the rest
of his days?

"JAKE! JAKE! DUDE, WAIT UP!"

Jake Montone heard his name but didn't bother slowing his steps as he strode down the middle of the crowded hall at the Village School, all the underclassmen instinctively moving out of his way. He wasn't in the habit of stopping for anyone. Except maybe the occasional beautiful girl. But Carlos Bernal could catch up with him.

Blister Busting

Besides, he didn't want to break concentration. It was tough to find a person in a crowd without appearing as if you were looking for someone. It took a special kind of control to cover up riveted attention with removed indifference.

"Hey, man, we have a problem," Carlos began when he fell into step with Jake, only slightly out of breath.

"Oh, yeah? What's that?" Jake asked. His eyes scanned the hallway, his mouth lifting ever so slightly whenever he caught the admiring glance of a lovely lady. He could have any girl in this place if he wanted. Unfortunately, that fact made him not want any of them.

"Rob Tesca has mono," Carlos announced, covering his mouth with his hand and pretending that he didn't want to laugh. Jake could tell he enjoyed being the bearer of this bad news.

"What?" Jake blurted, looking fully at Carlos for the first time. His hair was extra gelled today, and he looked like he'd just walked off the set of *Happy Days*, with his tight white T-shirt and the chain hanging off his jeans. The kid even had dimples.

"How the hell does a guy like Rob Tesca get mono?" Jake asked, the tendons in his neck tightening.

"Dude may be butt ugly, but he does do well with the ladies," Carlos replied, swerving around a klatch of gossiping freshmen and glancing behind his shoulder to check them out. "So what are we gonna do? The team is already hemorrhaging."

"Tell me about it," Jake said.

The intramural karate team that Jake had formed on arriving at this new school was not getting off to an auspicious start. A bunch of guys had shown up for the informational meeting, but it turned out that eighty percent of them had gleaned their martial arts expertise from hours of blister-busting Street Fighter tournaments they'd been having since the sixth grade. The talent pool in this place was so shallow, it wouldn't even wet a person's socks.

Jake caught a glimpse of a blond ponytail from the corner of his eye and almost paused, but it turned out to be one of those perky chicks who were always giggling every time he walked into a room. Not the blond he was looking for.

"So, anyway, what are we going to do?" Carlos asked.

Jake stepped out of traffic and paused near a row of lockers, rolling his eyes and expertly appearing as if he was simply fed up with the crush of people.

"I got an idea," Jake said, glancing left at the locker that belonged to the blond who he *was* looking for. The blond who, conveniently, could also solve this new problem.

"Yeah? What?" Carlos asked, gripping one strap of his backpack with both hands. "I'm all ears."

It was an unfortunate turn of phrase for a guy who was, in fact, mostly ears. Jake glanced from one of Carlos's big flappers to the other slowly, and Carlos reddened. It wasn't that Jake *wanted* to embarrass the kid. He actually kind of liked Carlos and his perpetual kinetic state. But if he were forced to reveal that Gaia Moore was the person he was thinking of to take Rob's spot, that she was the person he'd been scanning the halls for all day, that she was owner of the locker they'd just stopped next to, then he'd also be forced to admit something that he was not willing to admit.

That he couldn't stop thinking about her. That he wanted to spend more time with her. That the karate team was the perfect excuse.

"Why are we stopping here?" Carlos asked when he regained his happy-go-lucky self. "The bell's gonna ring."

"No reason," Jake said, shrugging one shoulder. He looked down the emptying hall, and there was no sign of her. Apparently Gaia had decided to take a vacation day. Jake tried to ignore the hot infusion of disappointment in his chest.

"Let's go," he said to Carlos, just as the bell rang.

He was not disappointed that he hadn't gotten to see her before homeroom. He wasn't. He just needed her. No. The *team* needed her. That's what this was all about.

And the fact that he'd been looking for her before he even knew the team needed her? *Eh.* That just meant he was psychic.

Friendless

THERE COMES A POINT IN EVERY MAN'S life when he has to ask himself, How did I get here. . . ? This, Ed Fargo, is that moment.

"Uh, you gonna move?"

Ed glanced over his shoulder at the scrawny little pale-faced, red-eyed Internet addict behind him and stepped out of his way. A group of four other such indoor beings, all of whom were probably still mourning the death of *The X-Files,* followed the kid out of the cafeteria line and over to a table in the corner.

See? Even geeky freshmen who haven't seen the sun since their diaper days have someone to sit with. You, however, have reached a point, as a senior, *where you do not. How did you* get *here?*

Taking a deep breath, Ed shuffled over to one of the smaller tables by the wall farthest from the lunch line, kicked a chair away from the table, and slumped into it. He placed his tray down in front of him and shrugged out of his backpack, tossing it into the empty chair to his right. It wasn't like anyone was going to be using it.

Ed picked up his plastic fork and stared at it `as if it held the meaning of life between its tines.` But his brain was actually trying to avoid finding the inevitable answer to his more pressing question by focusing on the inanimate object.

"I wonder why plastic forks grip pasta better," Ed muttered to himself, sticking the utensil into his noodles.

Unfortunately, this little quandary could only occupy his brain for so long, and the answer to the more important quandary finally came to him.

You got to this point because of Gaia, his brain voice said.

Ed's jaw clenched. No. That wasn't fair. It wasn't only Gaia's fault that he was `friendless`. It was Heather's, it was Tatiana's, it was... hormones. (Not to mention the fact that all his skate friends had scattered the moment he'd landed in his wheelchair and hadn't returned when he'd stepped out of it.) He'd spent the last few years, and the last few months especially, alienating everyone he knew in order to focus all his energy on women. Now all the women had up and left him, and he was friendless. It served him right.

A burst of laughter caught his attention, and he glanced over at the table in the center of the room that had welcomed the Friends of Heather at lunch hour every day of every year since they were but breastless, brace-faced fourteen-year-olds. Heather was no longer there, of course, but today Tatiana was missing as well. If she'd been there, then Ed might have sucked it up and gone over to sit with them and listen to them pick apart Jennifer Aniston's latest red carpet wear for forty-five minutes. At least then he wouldn't be sitting alone.

Of course, come to think of it, he might be better off where he was.

He realized, as he took his first bite of spaghetti, that he hadn't actually seen Tatiana all day. And Gaia was out as well—he'd noted that before the first bell. The dual absence couldn't be a coincidence. With those two, a simple flu was easy to rule out. They were probably back at home, kicking the crap out of each other. Not that he'd ever known Tatiana to be violent, but the way those two were acting around each other lately, it wouldn't have surprised him in the least.

Where the hell were they?

"Oh dear God, I have to get a life," Ed muttered, dropping his fork. He tipped back his head and covered his face with his hands, letting out a groan.

Enough with the Gaia obsession. Enough with the Tatiana "friendship" that could become something more. It had become clear to him over the past week or so that there was no way to be friends with Tatiana without constantly encountering Gaia, and he was never going to get over the girl if she was in his face all the time. And he had to get over her. It was for his own good. For his mental health. For his very survival.

Somehow, somewhere, there had to be a `normal girl` for Ed Fargo. Someone who didn't come with the lovely peripherals of gun-wielding psychos, vengeful thugs, and emotional issues too countless to list.

Why couldn't he find such a girl?

"Um... are you okay?"

Ed let his arms drop down and hang at his sides but barely moved his head. From the corner of his eye he could see a petite, pretty Asian girl in a pink-and-yellow T-shirt, with two short pigtails, tilting her head to look at him. She had a curious smile and a tiny diamond nose piercing.

"Yeah, I'm cool," Ed replied. He sat up straight and squeezed his eyes shut against the head rush.

"Oh, cuz you looked like you were a little... you know... floopy," she said, crinkling her nose. She was still holding her full lunch tray. She had a well-worn Birdhouse skateboard tucked under her arm.

"You skate street?" he asked semiblankly.

Her whole face lit up. "Yeah! And some vert," she said, setting down her tray and pulling out the board to show him. "This is my deck."

Ed frowned thoughtfully as he checked out the bird graphic on the bottom of the board, chipped away from hours of good, hard use.

"Nice," he said.

She grinned. Ed noticed that she had a nice smile. "Can I?" she said, gesturing at the chair across from his.

Ed barely lifted his shoulders. "Sure."

"I'm Kai," she said, shaking up her chocolate milk, her fifty rubber bracelets slipping up and down her arm.

"Ed," he replied.

"I've seen you skating down by Washington Square, right?" she asked.

"I've been known to," Ed replied, staring down at his food.

"You ever been to Extreme Skate up in Rhode Island?" Kai asked.

"No," Ed replied.

"Omigod, you have to go," Kai said, tearing into her salad. "I go every year, and it's the coolest jam on the East Coast, I swear. It's so not commercial, and when I was twelve, I entered the best trick contest and

I totally won, but not before I slammed, like, fifteen hundred times. . . ."

Ed smiled, but he felt himself starting to drift as Kai continued to talk about her many skateboarding exploits. He wondered where Gaia was at that very moment. Did she ever even think about him anymore? Did she realize she'd ruined him for life?

What if he would never be attracted to a normal girl again? Was this it for him? Was he going to have to date FBI chicks and cops and, like, vampire slayers or something for the rest of his days? At this point Ed wasn't even sure if he would recognize a normal girl if he found her.

"Are you sure you're okay?" Kai asked suddenly, ducking in toward the table to get into his line of vision.

"Yeah! Sorry," Ed said, pushing his hands through his thick black hair. "You were talking about Rhode Island. . . ?"

"Exactly! Like I said, you totally have to go. . . ."

Kai didn't seem fazed by his zone-out. Which was good, because it was probably going to happen again. He glanced around the cafeteria, looking in vain for some sign of Gaia or Tatiana, but they were definitely nowhere in sight. Something was going on. He could *feel* it. And he was going to find out what it was.

It wasn't like he had anything else to do—those girls had already destroyed his social life.

". . . we could go over to the park after school and I could show you, if you want," Kai said.

But Ed barely heard her. He was too busy planning the trip up to Seventy-second Street after school and what he would say to Gaia when he found her.

THE NURSE BEHIND THE COUNTER IN

Still Alive

the ICU looked up as Gaia walked out of the elevator and smiled a patented comforting smile, probably perfected after years of dealing with the families of the almost dead. Gaia glanced away, avoiding eye contact as she approached the woman. She didn't feel the need to be comforted. At least, not for the reason this woman thought she did. The patient Gaia was coming to see could stay in a coma until the hell he'd come from froze over, as far as she cared. She was probably the only person who'd ever come here hoping for "bad" news.

"Can I help you?" the nurse asked, lacing her fingers together as Gaia placed her bags on the floor in front of the chest-level desk.

"I'm here to see L—uh, Oliver. Oliver Moore," Gaia said.

The nurse's heavily lined eyes widened in surprise

and she stepped off her stool. "Really?" she said, sounding oddly happy. "Are you family?"

Gaia swallowed back the bile that rose in her throat. "Yeah. I'm his niece," she said, going for a smile but looking more like she wanted to throw up.

"Well! This is wonderful!" the nurse said, coming around the desk, her white sneakers squish-squashing as she walked. "Oliver never gets any visitors. We were beginning to wonder if he had anyone left. You see, the doctors like to have people come in and talk to our comatose patients. We always see better results when loved ones spend time talking and reading. . . ."

Gaia watched the nurse's face illuminate at the idea that poor old Oliver finally had someone who cared.

"Follow me," she said to Gaia as she squish-squashed toward the closed door to one of the rooms.

Gaia briefly considered turning around and bolting. The idea of actually laying eyes on the man who had made her life a relentless pit of pain wasn't appealing. But if there was one thing Gaia knew, it was that she should always make sure to see evidence with her own eyes. Whenever she was simply *told* something, nine and a half times out of ten it turned out to be untrue.

She picked up her bags again and followed the nurse over to the door she was now holding open. Gaia trudged up next to the woman and stood on the threshold, filling the empty doorway. There, lying flat on his back, was the man who was the spitting image of the father she'd loved and lost more times than she could count. Somewhere out there, if he was still alive, her father looked like an exact replica of the man lying before her. Hair combed back from his head, sensors pressed into his temples, arms placed neatly at his sides, machines beeping away all around him, stubble covering his strong chin.

In spite of all the hatred she felt, a huge lump welled up in Gaia's throat. She swallowed it back, ashamed of herself for displaying any kind of emotion at Loki's bedside. The nurse looked at her with pity in her eyes, and Gaia wanted to shake her and tell her the sorrow wasn't for Loki. No one should ever be sorry that this man was near death.

Okay, you've seen him, Gaia told herself. *Now go.*

"Talk to him," the nurse said softly. "It's okay."

No! Just leave! Gaia thought. But her legs wouldn't obey. As always, she was inexplicably drawn to Loki. And seeing him here like this. . . it somehow made her feel closer to her father.

The nurse slipped out, closing the door behind her and shutting out the light from the hallway. As soon as she and Loki were alone, Gaia's stomach clenched down to the size of a gum ball.

Swallowing hard, Gaia placed her bags down on the chair next to the door. She made her feet take the few necessary steps to the bed and stood there, her abdomen pressed into the metal railing that ran all around her uncle's resting place. He looked so vulnerable, lying there. Yet her fingers itched to circle his throat and squeeze out whatever life he had left. After everything this man had done to her and her family, he deserved to never wake up.

Like Dad, Gaia's mind blurted, as much as she tried to stop the thought from taking form. Loki and her father had always had that weird twin connection. They'd both fallen into comas at the same time. If it was really true that her father was dead, shouldn't Loki be, too?

Gaia's thoughts and emotions overwhelmed her. She pulled the second chair over to the bed and sat down, her knees weak. This was crazy, coming here. She should have known better. She should have left when her instincts told her to. But now it was too late. Everything she hadn't wanted to think about was hitting her full force.

Her father, her mother, Natasha and Tatiana's betrayal, her loneliness, her confusion, the fact that the only blood relative she might have left was not only evil but half dead in the bed in front of her. And the fact that it was now confirmed: She and her father had a new enemy. Someone other than Loki was out for their blood, and the only people who knew who that enemy was were Natasha and Tatiana. Gaia was back at square one.

"I don't know what to do," Gaia said, her throat

dry but her eyes full of tears she refused to shed. "I don't know what to do anymore."

The heart monitor bleeped away, and Gaia stared across the bed toward the shuttered window. Suddenly she laughed at herself. What was she doing here?

Gaia looked at his monitors. Lines peaked and dropped, dots jumped around. It all meant nothing to her. Nothing except that Loki was still breathing. And her father, for all she knew, was not.

"He's probably dead, you know," she heard herself say. Her gaze flicked toward Loki's face. "That should make you happy. I mean, that's what you always wanted, right? To kill your brother? To get your revenge? Well, I'm sorry you didn't get to do it yourself."

She glared at his face, waiting for a reaction she knew would never come. There was nothing more unsatisfying than trying to pick a fight with a guy in a coma. For once Gaia had nothing to punch, nothing to kick, no one to accuse. She had no recourse. And suddenly she felt very, very tired.

Gaia leaned back in her chair until the back of her head was resting on the top of the vinyl-covered cushion. It was warm in the hospital room, and the rhythmic beeping of the monitor was mesmerizing. Gaia could feel herself starting to slip into sleep and told herself to get up and go. She wouldn't keep vigil at her uncle's bedside.

But she was so tired. And she had no place to go.

And this chair was a hell of a lot more comfortable than that awful bench she'd slept on the night before. Maybe if she just took a little nap, she would wake up refreshed and be able to think more clearly.

Gaia had hardly even decided to let herself go when she fell into a deep, dreamless sleep.

GAIA AWOKE WITH A START. SHE looked around the hazy hospital room, momentarily confused but searching for the cause of her sudden consciousness. Her heart was racing from being jarred out of a resting rhythm, and she felt like someone had shouted in her ear or shoved her to wake her up. But there was nothing. Nothing but a prone Loki.

No Loki in Loki

Gaia sat up and stretched, letting out a wide yawn and enjoying the feeling of her muscles awakening— her joints cracking. However long she'd been out, it had been a good sleep, and as she blinked away her grogginess, she realized it was time to blow this Popsicle stand. Now that she was certain Loki was no threat to her and her father, she had to focus on Tatiana. She had work to do.

Standing up, Gaia started to gather her bags, but

then she saw something that made her stop short.

Loki's fingers moved. Gaia took an instinctive step back from the bed. Her eyes darted to the monitors, but as far as she could tell, nothing had changed. Maybe she'd just imagined the movement.

I did. I just imagined it, she told herself, watching the display of Loki's heartbeat as the line jumped and squiggled and faded away.

"G-Gaia?"

A sizzle of anger ran over Gaia's skin the moment she heard his voice. He was awake. The rat bastard was awake. And he was saying her name.

"Gaia... where... how did you...?"

And then he started coughing.

At first Gaia simply stood there, but the longer she did, the hoarser his coughing became. It racked his chest and sent his pulse skyrocketing. When he reached shakily for the protective bar around his bed, Gaia snapped to and rushed out the door.

"Hey! I need some water in here!" she shouted, causing the nurse to jump out of her chair.

Gaia waited for the nurse to scurry into action, then returned to Loki's room, watching as the coughs shook his body and praying that he wouldn't choke before she had the chance to tell him how much she hated him.

The nurse rushed in with a pitcher of water and

poured Loki a cup. She leaned over the bed and helped him drink, supporting his head with her hand. Gaia cringed just watching someone else touch the bastard. If only this woman knew what he had done.

"Better?" the nurse said when Loki had downed the water.

Loki nodded and lay down again weakly.

"His throat will be very dry," the nurse said, turning to Gaia. As if Gaia cared. "All those days with nothing to moisten it."

"Right," Gaia said. "You don't seem that surprised he's awake."

"Well, there have been indications in the past few days that something like this might happen," the nurse said. "More color in the cheeks, strengthening of the brain waves." She turned around and smiled at Loki, who was staring up at the ceiling with a confused expression. "But I wouldn't be surprised if you're the reason he's coming out of it now," the nurse continued. "Familial support has a very powerful effect on coma patients."

How about the familial support from the niece who wants you dead? Gaia thought.

"I'm going to go alert his doctor," the nurse told Gaia, handing her the water pitcher. "You should talk to him, but try not to excite him. He's still very weak."

Then, with a joyous I'm-so-happy-for-you glance, the nurse hurried away.

"Gaia," Loki croaked the second the nurse was gone.

Gaia didn't move. He turned his head and looked up into her eyes. Gaia didn't want to look at him, but something in his face made her pause. She couldn't tear her gaze away. It seemed like his eyes had softened. The hard, sadistic laughing that had always been present was gone. He gazed at her with admiration, with love. At that moment there was no *Loki* in Loki.

It's just the medication, Gaia told herself, turning away to place the pitcher on the nightstand. *He's totally drugged, that's all.*

"Well, you should get some rest," Gaia said, wiping her sweaty palms on her cargo pants. "I'll just leave you alone."

"Gaia, wait!" he exclaimed in his hoarse voice. "Why am I here?"

The sizzle of anger returned, this time heating Gaia's very veins. "You were in a coma. You woke up," she told him, grabbing up her bags. "The nurses will fill you in."

"But I. . . I don't remember anything," he said, blinking rapidly. "I don't. . . understand. How did I get here? When?"

After you tried to kill me and *Heather* and *my father,* Gaia's inner voice shouted.

"Look, you were in a *coma,*" Gaia said bitingly. "It may take you a little while to remember some things, but you will. Take care."

"But Gaia—"

"I am not going to help you. Not this time," Gaia said, her eyes flashing dangerously. "Not after everything you did. And don't give me any of that 'But I'm your uncle' bull, because I'm done falling for it."

She turned to leave and had her hand on the door handle when he spoke again.

"But Gaia, I *am* your uncle. It's me, Oliver!" From the sound of his voice he was near tears. Gaia's heart pounded in her chest. "Please don't leave me here. I don't understand what's happened!"

He collapsed in another coughing fit. Gaia turned slowly to find him reaching out for the water, unable to grasp it from his position, his arms shaking from the strain of stretching them. She narrowed her eyes.

Don't believe him, she told herself. *Believing him has gotten you into trouble so many times. . . .*

But then, from what she understood about human physiology, any trauma to the brain can change a person's emotional makeup. And a coma can cause trauma to the brain.

It can't be, Gaia thought.

But what if he *was* just Oliver? If he really was Oliver, she couldn't just leave him here to rot alone. If he really was Oliver, maybe he could help her.

Gaia dropped her things and poured him another glass of water. He drank it thirstily and collapsed back into his pillow. As he fought for his breath, Gaia watched him carefully. Loki was, after all, a fine actor.

He'd fooled her many, many times. And Gaia didn't want to be fooled again.

"Gaia, please don't leave me here," Oliver said, his chest rising and falling fast. "Take me home with you."

Gaia crossed her arms over her chest and dug her fingers into her biceps. "I don't have a home."

His eyes traveled past her then, and he seemed to notice her bags for the first time.

"But. . . what about your father?" Oliver asked.

Gaia's jaw clenched and her eyes stung. How was she supposed to answer that question? Especially when she didn't even know who she was talking to— someone who would rejoice in the news or someone who would be devastated?

"He's. . . missing," Gaia said finally.

Oliver quickly looked away, blinking rapidly as he stared up at the ceiling. Because of the line of work Tom was in, the fact that he was MIA wouldn't come as too much of a shock. But to a brother, if that was who he was, it was still upsetting.

If he's Loki, he deserves an Oscar, Gaia thought.

When her uncle turned to look at her again, his expression was resolved. "Where. . . what city are we in?" he asked.

"New York," she replied.

"I have a place, then," he said. "A place we can go." His frail fingers grasped at the metal guardrail closest to her. "I can't stay here, Gaia. I don't trust hospitals."

He swallowed with difficulty and pulled in a breath. "Ever since I was a little boy. . ."

Gaia felt an infinitesimal tug at her heart. She knew the feeling. And she knew what Oliver had gone through as a boy—all that time in and out of medical facilities, all those tests. If he was Oliver, he had every right to be petrified.

Still, how could she even think about taking him out of here? If he was actually Loki, she'd be unleashing some major evil.

"I know you have no reason to trust me. I don't remember what got me here yet, but I do remember the things I've done to you in the past. . . as Loki," Oliver said. "But I'll prove to you I'm not Loki. . . somehow. And if I don't prove it, you have every right to kill me."

Damn straight, Gaia thought.

She took a deep breath and looked into the man's desperate, scared eyes. Suddenly she knew she was going to do it—she was going to break Loki or Oliver, whoever he was, out of here. Maybe it was a serious lapse in judgment, but the fact remained that whichever personality had emerged from the coma, he was still the only person she knew who might be able to help her find her dad. If he turned out to be Loki, well, then, he was right—she would just have to deal with him.

Gaia walked over to the door, opened it a crack, and glanced out. Another nurse had taken charge of the desk while the first woman was off paging Loki's doctor. There was a doctor talking to a harried-looking couple outside another of the rooms. It wasn't Fort Knox, but it wasn't going to be easy. She closed the door again, silently.

"They'll never let me take you out of here in this condition," she said, glancing skeptically at his frail body. "We're gonna have to run."

TATIANA STILL COULDN'T GET USED TO

Dead Ahead

seeing all those dark strands of hair blowing in front of her own face. Every other time the wind kicked up and tousled her wig, she flinched. Not exactly the nerves of steel required for the spy game. But she'd been following Gaia all day, and since the girl seemed to be able to function indefinitely without food, Tatiana hadn't eaten, either. She leaned her shoulder against the big blue mailbox next to her and tapped her fingers on the dented metal, her stomach letting out an irritated growl. She was starting to get a little antsy.

"What the hell is she doing in there, having that long overdue personality change operation?" Tatiana muttered, glancing away from the hospital entrance long enough to check her watch. Gaia had been inside for more than two hours. A new record of stagnancy for the day. Maybe Tatiana could just duck into that bagel place and—

There she was. Not coming from the entrance, but from around the far corner of the hospital. And she was hustling. She was hustling with her arm around someone. Someone who was stooped over and shielded from view. Tatiana stood up straight, pulled her dark sunglasses down to the end of her nose, and narrowed her eyes.

Who the hell was Gaia smuggling out of the damn—

The patient glanced in her direction, only for a split second, and Tatiana's knees almost caved in. Tom Moore? Gaia's *father?* But how had she—? How had he—? She'd thought he was—

Then it hit her, and a dry heave caught in her throat.

It wasn't Tom. It was Loki, obviously. Tatiana and her mother had known for a while that Loki was being held in one of the city's many hospitals, but the name of the exact hospital was kept on a need-to-know basis. And even though it made absolutely no sense for Gaia to smuggle Loki out of the hospital, it made more sense than the idea of Tom being in New York. Tatiana knew for a fact that Tom was nowhere near the United States.

This can't happen, Tatiana realized, her heart racing. If Gaia and Loki had decided to team up, there was no telling what they might be able to do. And if the two of them compared notes, it wouldn't take long for them to figure out who Tatiana and Natasha were working for. Once they figured that out, Tatiana was as good as dead. Especially if she could have done something to stop it.

Gaia and her uncle scurried across the avenue and headed toward Tatiana but on the other side of the street. Tatiana ducked behind a lamppost, seething, swearing under her breath.

"I'll kill them," she said. "I'll kill them both."

Gaia and Loki turned a corner and started up the street toward the subway station, their backs to Tatiana. Suddenly a sleek black sports car pulled up to the curb right next to Tatiana's feet and the engine died. Tatiana squared her shoulders, walked around the front of the car, and waited for the driver to open the door.

A coiffed businessman of about thirty stepped out onto the street, his back to Tatiana. She reached around him, took his keys from his hand, and, before he could utter any sound of surprise, grabbed him by his jacket lapels and flung him to the ground.

As she sat behind the wheel and locked the doors, Tatiana absently noticed that now her hands weren't shaking. They weren't shaking as she inserted the key into the ignition. They weren't shaking as she cut the wheel and peeled out, slicing through four lanes of heavy New York traffic.

The driver stood up and yelled after her; countless cars screeched to a stop; curses were flung out like yesterday's meat loaf. But Tatiana didn't hear them. She didn't see them. She saw nothing but the tall blond girl and the sickly, stooped man, who were so helpfully stepping off the curb and into the street dead ahead.

You know what's unhealthy?
Giving up stuff for a girl.

Like when I was in high
school, my friend Frank quit the
spring play because his girlfriend, Lily, was jealous because
he had to kiss Maria Viola. Then
five days after we all watched
Frank's understudy, Calvin
Carmichael, knock over the set
and pass out from an asthma
attack in the middle of act 2,
Lily broke up with Frank for some
kid from the debate team. Frank
never acted again, never trusted
women again, and took his first
cousin Agatha to the prom. I
haven't spoken to him since, but
I'm sure he's still a shell of
his former self.

It's because of the Frank and
Lily story that I'm in New York
at all. I had a girlfriend in
high school. An amazing girlfriend. Her name was Anna, and
she was perfect—smart, funny,
legs that went on for miles. We
always used to lie around and

talk about what it would be like to go away to school together, live together, and all that stuff. But Anna wanted to go to Notre Dame more than anything. Her whole family went there. Their den was like a shrine to the place, with pennants and jackets and photos, pillows, blankets, and mugs. I applied there, but I knew that I didn't want to stay in the Midwest. I knew I wanted to go to school in a big city, see new things, get the heck out of small-town USA.

And so, when I got my acceptance letters to NYU and Notre Dame on the same day and immediately went for the one from NYU first, I knew what I had to do. I thought about Frank. I thought about how I didn't want to make that same mistake he had. So I broke Anna's heart and I came to New York.

The thing is, I never looked back. Yeah, I still think of Anna sometimes, but I know that I made the right decision. And not just because she got engaged to some prelaw loser six months into her freshman year (I got an e-mail from her with their engagement picture attached. They were both wearing Notre Dame sweatshirts and green turtlenecks), but because I've always believed that you've got to make your own decisions. Like I said, you can't give up stuff for a girl.

So what do you do when you've given up not just your hobby for a girl, but *everything*? You've given up your friends, your passions, your education, your family, and approximately three full months of your life? And then what do you do if, after you've given up all that, she decides that you aren't worth trusting? That everything you've done and everything you've lost doesn't even prove that one small thing. How does one recover from that?

Need a few minutes to think about it? That's cool, I'll wait. It's not like I have anything else to do.

And at that moment, she knew. She knew, without a doubt, that this was truly Oliver.

the good guys

OKAY, WHAT THE HELL AM I DOING HERE?

Quiver

Gaia asked herself, glancing at her uncle's profile as she half dragged him along the street. The light of day and the noise of the streets were like blaring wake-up calls from the intense emotional daze back in the hospital room. Sure, this man claimed his name was Oliver Moore, and he didn't seem to recall anything he'd done in the days before he fell into a coma. Sure, he looked pale and weak and his arms shook as he clasped her left hand in both of his.

But none of this changed the fact that she might have just sprung the most evil criminal on earth from the hospital. Loki was a chameleon. That was one of his strengths as a spy. And although Gaia's gut was telling her to believe that the person she was holding up was Oliver, her gut had betrayed her enough times for her to be doubtful.

She was so sick of doing this alone—of relying on her own instincts. If only she had someone here to tell her she was doing the right thing. Or the wrong one. Either way, she could deal. She just wanted to *know*.

"Oh God, no," Oliver said suddenly, stopping so fast, Gaia almost pulled him off his feet with her continued momentum. Oliver turned, spinning himself out of her grasp. He started to fall and grabbed at a grimy, overflowing garbage can to stop himself.

"What is it?" Gaia asked, glancing left and right.

65

She doubted the nurses had even noticed that Oliver was missing from his room yet, but if Loki's men had been keeping an eye on the hospital, they might already be tailing her. It was always better to be safe than dead.

Oliver looked at her, his blue eyes swimming and twitching, his mouth hanging slightly open. He slowly sank to the ground, every muscle in his body seeming to quiver.

"I—tried to—kill you?" Oliver stammered, tucking his chin.

Any color he had left drained from his face. Gaia felt her stomach turn over like a slowly folding omelette. Was he serious?

"Uh. . . yeah," Gaia said, trying to prevent the emotion she felt from creeping into her voice. "Lots of times. But we can talk about that later."

She grabbed his arms around what was left of his biceps and tried to haul him up, but he was like deadweight. His fluttering hand flew to his forehead and he squeezed his eyes shut.

"And that girl Heather. . . and Tom. . . my own brother. . . and that boy. . . that boy. . . Josh. . . I killed him at point-blank. . ."

And then Oliver started to weep. Sitting right there on the ground in the middle of a crowded sidewalk, with harried pedestrians looking him over warily as they hustled by. Gaia stood still, unsure of what to do—unsure of what she was witnessing. Everything that had happened before Loki had slipped into his coma seemed to be coming back to him, slowly and in agonizing relief. With each new victim he recalled, he collapsed in on himself a bit more.

So it was all coming back to him. But was it coming back to him as Oliver, or were his memories turning him back into Loki, the man who had actually committed those atrocities?

"Oh God, why did you take me out of there?" her uncle whimpered, covering his face with both hands now. "You must despise me. You have to despise me...."

I do, Gaia thought. *Or I did. I despise Loki. So if that's who you are...*

Car tires screeched somewhere down the street and Gaia blinked. She had to snap out of this. They both had to.

"Look, we can talk about all of this later?" she asked, grasping his hands and hauling him to his feet. She wrapped her arm around his back, supporting his weight, and started to walk. "Right now we just need to get you inside, okay?"

Oliver didn't respond, but he did move with her, muttering under his breath. Mercifully Gaia could no longer comprehend his muddled words. If she heard him recount his memory of what he'd done to her mother, she might just give in to temptation and leave him right on a street corner to fend for himself.

"Come on. We have to cross here," she said, tightening her grip on his shoulder.

As Gaia stepped from the curb, Oliver paused again. Gaia stopped a few paces ahead of him, in the center of the road. She was starting to lose patience.

"Are you coming?" she asked him.

A fat tear rolled down the side of Oliver's nose and his chin quivered. He looked so entirely pathetic—so scared and remorseful. Gaia swallowed back a lump that threatened to rise in her throat. If this really was Oliver, he must be so confused. Of course, if he was Loki, he was just doing a really good job of snowing her. And he wouldn't be the first.

Suddenly Oliver, Loki, whoever he was swayed on his feet. Gaia took a step toward him, then froze.

The sound of screeching tires filled her ears this time, impossibly close. Gaia looked up to see a black sports car almost spin out as it flew around the nearest corner. The driver was obscured, but as the engine roared and picked up speed, it was clear he wasn't going to stop. Gaia was standing directly in the car's path.

Huh. In all the times she'd imagined herself dying, getting run over by a car was never at the top of the list.

"Gaia!" Oliver shouted suddenly.

Then, before Gaia could even turn to him, he'd run into the center of the street and shoved her out of the way of the speeding car, his eyes wild. Gaia hit the road on her butt, her palms scraping across the grainy asphalt.

When she looked up at her uncle, he was standing in the path of the car, his arms outstretched at his sides.

"No!" Gaia shouted, scrambling up.

As clear as day, she heard her uncle state, ever so simply, "I deserve to die."

And at that moment she knew. She knew without a doubt that this was truly her uncle, her father's brother, the man her mother once knew and cared for. He was one of the good guys.

Gaia glanced at the car, only yards away now and coming fast. A jogger jumped out of the vehicle's way, tumbling over the hood of a parked Jeep. The black car only accelerated. Whoever was behind the wheel either didn't know or didn't care that he had almost killed someone.

And that meant her uncle was next. Out of the corner of her eye Gaia caught a glimpse of long dark hair and dark glasses behind the wheel of the speeding car. Then she took off, using the few steps to gain as much momentum as superhumanly possible. She launched herself into the air and slammed into her uncle, wrapping her arms around him as they tumbled toward the far curb. They rolled over and over each other, legs entwined, arms flailing, until the curb stopped Gaia's back, sending a stabbing, body-shaking pain down her side.

The car didn't pause or slow. When Gaia lifted her head, it had already disappeared into traffic.

"Hey! Are you all right?" A burly man in an orange

Con Edison vest crouched over them on the sidewalk.

Gaia sat up slowly, touching a cut on her head and wincing as she glanced around at the crowd that had gathered. Her uncle started to cough, and Gaia helped him into a seated position, checking him over for broken bones. He was clearly shaken but still intact.

"We're fine," Gaia said to the little clutch of people. "Thanks."

"Wacko," the Con Edison worker said under his breath. "I tried to get his license plate, but it all happened so fast."

"Thanks again," Gaia said as the man stood up and walked off, shaking his head.

As the rest of the bystanders started to disperse, Oliver got his breathing under control. He looked over at Gaia and blinked rapidly.

"You saved my life," he said. "Why?"

Gaia shrugged. "You saved mine first."

Oliver looked down at his hands as if he couldn't believe they were there. "Back in the hospital, you said that Tom was. . . missing?"

Gaia's heart turned. "Yep," she said, pretending to concentrate on dabbing the blood from the scrape above her eye with the end of her sleeve.

"But he's alive," Oliver said.

"I don't know," Gaia replied.

Oliver let out a breath, and his shoulders slumped a bit more. "Well, wherever he is, I'll find him," he said. "I'm going to put a stop to all of this. Once and for all."

Gaia turned her head to look at him, and Oliver looked right back into her eyes. She wanted to believe him so badly—believe that he was really going to help her. But even if he really was Oliver, how long would he stay that way?

After all, Loki hadn't been born. He was a product of Oliver's bottomless self-hatred.

ED HAD NEVER SEEN SUCH A PATHETIC

Good Progress

display of athleticism in his life. There were four girls on the two racquetball courts that the school gymnasium could accommodate, and they all sucked. He hadn't seen a good volley yet. Mostly one girl hit the ball at the wall, it came flying back, the other girl screeched and ducked out of the way, and then the first girl had to chase the ball down. Then the whole process started over again. The guys sitting in the bleachers above him seemed to find it entertaining, but all Ed could think about was the fact that these were forty-five minutes of his life that he would never get back.

And that if Gaia were here, she'd be putting all the other girls to shame.

Damn. He wasn't supposed to be thinking like that.

"Hey, Fargo!"

Ed turned around to find Jake Montone lumbering down the bleachers toward him with Carlos Bernal in tow. The skin on Ed's bare arms flared with heat at the sight of him, and he turned to face the courts again, feigning such sudden intense interest, he could have been a college racquetball scout.

"S'up, man?" Jake said, standing a couple of rows down from Ed so that he couldn't avoid looking at him in his gray T-shirt with the sleeves ripped off. Carlos waited for Jake down on the gym floor, keeping one eye on the racquetball players for his own safety.

"Nothing," Ed replied.

"Where's the little woman today?" Jake asked.

Ed pulled in a deep breath. "What little woman would that be?" he asked.

Jake laughed. "You know—belligerent chick with a nice big man-shaped chip on her shoulder?"

"Belligerent! Big word!" Ed snapped, in order to cover the surge of jealousy that threatened to overtake him. What the hell did this guy want with Gaia? And exactly how many guys did Ed's ex have lined up for herself, anyway? Sam, Jake... who was next?

"All I did was ask you a question," Jake said, an edge creeping into his tone.

"Well, all I know is she's not here," Ed said, lifting his feet and placing them on the step in front of him. "Out of curiosity, why do you ask?" he added, forcedly casual. It wasn't like he *really* wanted to know the answer. And it wasn't like he wanted Jake to think that he cared. But sometimes his tongue just felt the need to set him up for punishment.

"Not that it's any of your business, but I have something to ask her," Jake replied. Then he turned and loped down the rest of the bleachers, walking with Carlos over to the far court to take their turn with the rackets.

What do you have to ask her? Ed wanted to shout after him. *Is this like a help-me-with-my-homework-so-I-can-look-up-your-skirt question or a go-with-me-to-the-prom-so-I-can-put-my-hand-in-your-blouse question?!*

But Jake was right about one thing: It *was* none of his business. Ed knew this. He had to stop obsessing about Gaia and what she was doing and who she was doing it with. This behavior was going to get him nowhere.

Unfortunately, it was tough to teach an old Ed new tricks. And he'd spent so much time focused on Gaia in the last year, it was going to be difficult to break himself of the habit. Perhaps impossible.

Ed picked at a string sticking out from the leather upper on his sneaker, wishing he had something else, anything else, to focus on. He'd thought dating someone new would be the answer, but the further the school day progressed, the clearer it became that there was no one out there for him. This school was just too damned small. He'd been friends with every girl in it since his paste-eating days. And sure, there was a whole big city out there, but what was he going to do, go down to SoHo and pick up random chicks? The whole point of getting away from Gaia was to *keep* from getting his life threatened. Well, that was one of the points, anyway.

Maybe he should join a club. Or. . . or get a pet. Yeah, that was it. A dog. Or a nice cat. Yeah. Cats were cool. And then he could train it and feed it and it would cuddle up next to him at night and—

Yeah. Okay. Now he was thinking like a seventy-five-year-old woman. Good progress.

"Hey, Ed!"

He looked up from his sneaker to find Jennifer Niccols standing on the gym floor directly below him. Her curly brown hair was tied up in a high ponytail, and she was wearing a pair of short blue gym shorts that might as well have been underwear for all the area they covered.

"I need a partner," she said, flashing a toothpaste-commercial smile. "Wanna play?"

She took two rackets from behind her back and held one out toward him.

"I don't know," Ed replied, finding it difficult to

imagine himself out of wallow mode. Especially as far out as he'd have to be to get up the energy for racquetball. "I'm not really in the mood."

"Oh, come on," Jennifer said. She put the rackets down and climbed the bleachers until she was one riser in front of him. "What if I said pretty please?"

She cocked her head to one side and pretended to pout, reminding Ed of the time in kindergarten she'd proposed marriage to him in the Housekeeping Corner. Yet another girl he'd known for way too long. They were like brother and sister to each other.

Back then, of course, Ed had given in to her girlish wiles and ended up with his first kiss on the playground later that day.

He still blushed just thinking about it.

"Yes!" Jennifer said, noting the change in his coloring. She grabbed both his hands and pulled him out of his seat.

Ed followed her down the bleachers and picked up the racket, then swung his arm around and around, loosening up. It actually felt pretty good to move. Maybe this wasn't such a bad idea. Maybe smacking a ball around would get out some of his pent-up emotion. And maybe participating in gym would take his mind off his total lack of potential girlfriends for a little while.

But later he was definitely going to get a cat.

TATIANA LIFTED THE SMUDGED GLASS

of vodka from the bar, and half the contents sloshed over the rim onto her hand. She cursed under her breath and put the glass down again with a smack, attracting the attention of the surly bartender who was devouring the want ads at the other end of the counter.

"You gonna drink that or wipe down my bar with it?" he spat, one cheek so full of chewing tobacco, he looked like he had mumps.

Tatiana narrowed her eyes, steeled herself to stop her shaking hands, and downed the rest of the drink. She closed her eyes and tipped back her head as it burned down her throat, then immediately felt better.

At least she hadn't done it. Or, in truth, at least she'd been prevented from doing it by the tag-team heroics of what was left of the Moore family. And at least there were seedy, no-name bars open in this city in the middle of the afternoon—bars that didn't bother to card as long as you had cash. At least she'd been able to ditch the car and disappear.

Tatiana took a deep breath and leaned her elbows on the rough edge of the chipped wooden bar. She couldn't believe she'd just come so close to eliminating Gaia—the one person who knew how Tatiana could get her mother back.

But why did Gaia get Loki out of the hospital?
Tatiana wondered. *Why did she save one of her enemies from death?*

Tatiana lifted her hand to signal the bartender, and he quickly poured her another drink. As she took another hot swallow, she realized that only one thing in this life was certain—she would never figure out Gaia Moore. But that didn't mean she couldn't use her.

I have to get her to tell me what she knows, Tatiana thought. But if there was one thing that her near encounter with Gaia today had proved, it was that there was no way Tatiana could ever hope to take her. It wasn't as if she hadn't known this before, but watching Gaia throw herself across the street in front of a speeding car had just brought the point home for Tatiana. Gaia was practically a superhero. Tatiana couldn't rely on her own strength to deal with her. She had to find someone to help her—preferably someone with a little firepower. And that was the other reason that bars like this one were so handy—they were full of shady characters.

Tatiana lifted her finger again. The bartender sighed heavily, spat a wad of tobacco into a decaying glass, then trudged over to her.

"You ready to settle up?" he asked.

"Actually, I have a little trouble that I thought you might help me with," she said, calling upon the broken English she spoke only days after immigrating to the U.S.

Her trouble with the language made her seem helpless, and guys like this bartender were often more inclined to notice a damsel in distress.

He seemed to notice her for the first time and smiled back, his teeth yellow and gapped. Apparently he wasn't the type of person who saw smiles very often.

"What kind of trouble could a lady like you have?" he asked, clicking his tongue.

"It is my husband," Tatiana said, the lie dripping off her tongue. "He does not know how to stay at home, you know? I need to find someone who will teach him." Tatiana filled her eyes with meaning and stared at the greasy man. "Do you know of anyone who might help me?"

The bartender stood up straight and looked around the nearly empty bar. He picked up a damp rag and fiddled with it as he weighed whether or not to trust her. Tatiana leaned into the bar, letting the sleeve of her wide-necked sweater slip down slightly to expose her bra strap. The man's eyes were riveted.

"I may know someone, but it'll cost ya," he said.

"Money is no problem," Tatiana replied.

The bartender looked her up and down. "Be here tomorrow at noon," he said. "Brendan'll be here then. He's the one ya wanna talk to."

Brendan, Tatiana thought, smiling her thanks. She took a long, slow pull on her drink. *Let's just hope Brendan has a few friends. . . .*

I've decided to take this girl search very seriously. Why? Because one, I have no life and so I have time to take the search as seriously as I want. Two, if I find a girl, I will have a life and therefore will have remedied that problem. And three, I can't get a cat. I forgot that I'm allergic.

So where does one go to find cool girls in the city of New York?

1. Chelsea Piers. Pro: active chicks. Con: chicks who think that Chelsea Piers is the coolest place in Manhattan.

2. Bowlmor. Pro: chicks who can bowl. Con: chicks who can bowl better than me.

3. CBGB. Pro: musical chicks. Con: scary musical chicks.

4. The Guggenheim. Pro: cultured chicks. Con: boring chicks who can spend hours dissecting the meaning of a red blob on a canvas.

~~5. Washington Square Park.~~

6. The School of the Performing Arts. Pro: *Fame* chicks. Con: chicks with stage moms.

7. The Strand, half-priced-books section. Pro: chicks that not only read but know where to find a good bargain. Con: chicks that think you're Satan if you've ever been inside a Barnes & Noble.

8. Paragon. Pro: sporty chicks. Con: chicks who will spend two hundred bucks on a backpack.

9. The observation deck at the Empire State Building. Pro: international chicks. Con: too *Sleepless in Seattle*.

10. Port Authority. Pro: opens up the field to chicks from Jersey and Connecticut. Con: also opens up the field to hookers.

Once Jake
knew what he
wanted, he
went **falling**
after it,
and usually
he got it.

GAIA STEPPED OUT OF THE SUBWAY

station in the West Village and took a deep breath. The weak morning sunlight glinted in the window of a tiny shoe repair shop, and a man in a stained white apron blasted the sidewalk with water from

Chocolaty Goodness

a coiled hose. It was a new day. Gaia had come to school via a whole new route, leaving from Oliver's creaky, dirty brownstone in Brooklyn. Different subway platform, different train, different people. It was weird how seeing the world from a new angle could give a person a whole new outlook. And this morning Gaia felt strangely positive. She was going to figure out the meaning of the key she'd found at the Seventy-second Street apartment. She was going to find Tatiana. And Oliver was going to find her father. Everything was going to be fine.

As long as Loki didn't resurface. As long as Tatiana didn't find Gaia first and put a bullet through her head. As long as her father wasn't dead.

Gaia glanced across the street at the Village School and saw Jake Montone hanging on the steps with a couple of his meathead friends and a few Friends of Heather. Maybe one of them could help her find Tatiana. Maybe Tatiana had slipped up during one of their little gatherings and said something, *anything* that could give Gaia a clue. Of course, it wasn't like any of them were ever going to help her voluntarily. None of them would even *speak* to her voluntarily.

Unless she planned to intimidate each one of them, she was going to need a different in.

Suddenly Jake looked up and caught Gaia watching them. His amazingly light eyes grabbed her attention, even from that distance, and Gaia glanced away a second later than she would have liked.

"Damn," she muttered under her breath when she noticed the self-satisfied smirk that crossed his face. Ugh! He thought she was checking him out. Just what she needed—Mr. Ego thinking he had yet another admirer.

Gaia turned and ducked into Dunkin' Donuts with a sigh. Her positive mood had lasted all of ten minutes. Now she needed a double-chocolate doughnut and a nice big black coffee to take the edge off.

She joined the long line of half-asleep workers and scanned the shelves behind the counter, making sure there were double-chocolate doughnuts to be had. She smiled when a guy came out from the back wearing his maroon-and-orange Dunkin' uniform and carrying a whole new tray of `chocolaty goodness`. Maybe this really was her lucky day.

"Hey, Gaia."

Maybe not. She turned in line to find Jake standing behind her with that somehow constantly teasing smile on his face. So predictable. He thought she wanted him, so he came right after her. He was wearing a dark blue T-shirt and no jacket, even though everyone else in line was bundled up against the morning chill. He was bending and unbending a tattered copy of *Atlas Shrugged* in his large hands. Gaia noticed this, scoffed, and turned around again to focus on the task at hand—doughnut acquisition.

"What? Surprised by my choice of reading material?" Jake asked, inching closer to her as the line moved forward.

"Surprised you read," Gaia replied, her back to him.

Jake laughed. "Set myself up for that one."

"At least you can admit it," Gaia replied.

"So. . . you weren't in school yesterday," Jake said, angling himself so that he could see her profile as she stepped up to the counter. He leaned in near the cash register and rested his elbow on top of it, earning a `fire-spouting glare` from the lady behind the counter.

"Thanks for the news flash," Gaia said to him.

"Can I help you?" the lady asked through her teeth. She glanced at Jake again, but he didn't notice.

"I'll have a large coffee, black, and a double chocolate," Gaia said. Her stomach grumbled. "Make that two double chocolates."

Out of the corner of her eye she saw Jake smile but refused to give him the satisfaction of acknowledging it.

"And another black coffee," Jake piped up suddenly as the woman turned to fill the order. She rolled her eyes, made a big show of punching the extra coffee into the register, and hit total before grabbing a couple of large cups.

"I'm not buying you coffee," Gaia said to Jake as she fished in the pocket of her cargo pants for some cash.

"Nooooo," he said as if he were speaking to a four-year-old. He pushed away from the counter and pulled a sleek black wallet out of the back pocket of his fitted jeans. "I'm buying you coffee. And a couple of dough-nuts, apparently."

He slipped out a brand-new twenty and tossed it onto the counter. Gaia could actually smell the crispy scent of freshly printed bills. What was this kid, a Soprano or something?

"That's okay, really," she said, snapping up the twenty between two fingers and handing it back to him. "I don't really feel the need to owe you."

"You won't owe me," he said, throwing the money on the counter again. "God! I'm just trying to be nice. What are you, allergic to nice?"

Huh. . . maybe, Gaia thought, mulling it over. *That would explain a lot.*

The Dunkin' Donuts lady placed a waxy bag on the counter next to two steaming cups of coffee and, before Gaia could protest, picked up the twenty and started hitting buttons again. Jake smirked as he leaned past Gaia to pick up his cup. His arm grazed her cheek and she turned away from him, the contact sending an unexpected thrill the skittering down her side.

For a split second Gaia held her breath, then her face flushed purple. Because against her will she realized she was wishing that little skin brush had lasted longer.

Okay, you are not attracted to Jake Montone, she told herself, even though her fluttery stomach was insisting otherwise. *You're obviously just delusional from stress.*

Gaia snatched up her bag of doughnuts, slid past Jake, avoiding the merest brush of contact, and pushed the door to the shop open so hard it almost came off its hinges. The second she was outside, she opened the bag and broke off half of one of the doughnuts, still warm from the oven. She stuffed it into her mouth as she crossed the street against the signal.

Maybe if she kept walking, he'd take the hint. Maybe if she kept walking, her skin would cool down and her brain would start functioning again and realize that Jake Montone was so not her type. Not only that, but even if he *was* her type, this was no time to be thinking about guys on any level—unless they were guys who could help her find her dad.

"Hey!" Jake called out behind her.

Just let him get hit by a bus, Gaia thought.

"Hey! Don't I even get a thank-you?" He was closer now, coming up on her heels.

Gaia chewed and swallowed and turned to face him. "I don't remember asking you to buy me breakfast," she said. *See! You're looking right at him and feeling nothing. It was just a blip.*

He eyed that little white bag in her hand. "Using the term *breakfast* rather loosely."

Gaia rolled her eyes and was on the move again. What was he going to do now, lecture her about the four basic food groups?

"Waitwaitwait," Jake said, grabbing her arm. Gaia's heart thumped and she sighed. "I actually wanted to ask you something."

Oh God, he's not going to ask me out on a date, is he? I look like a hellion. Does he not have eyes?

Gaia had, in fact, showered for the first time in a number of days that morning, but she'd only had time to wrap her hair up in a folded-over ponytail, with straggly wisps sticking out in all directions. Her cargo pants were covered with stains and her white ribbed sweater had such deep creases in it, she wasn't sure if they were ever coming out. Add that to the fact that she was, as always, makeupless and jewelryless and that her denim jacket smelled like street urchin, and she was sure she didn't paint a pretty picture.

"I. . . uh. . . I wanted to ask you if. . . you would consider. . ."

Okay, whatever it is, spit it out, Gaia thought.

"If you would consider joining the karate team," Jake finished.

Gaia's heart squeezed, and she felt her face fall. *What?* But no. She was not disappointed. She was relieved, right? Thank *God!*

"You already asked me that and I already said no," Gaia replied. She clumsily opened the little flap on the plastic coffee cup top, spilling droplets on her hands, then took a sip.

"I know, but one of the guys got sick and I really need someone to take his place or we'll have to forfeit," Jake said. He raised his dark eyebrows. "Come on, Gaia. The team needs you."

There was a persuasive argument. "I don't think so," she said. She started off toward school again, double time.

"Come on! How could you not want to do this?" Jake asked, falling into step with her. "You love to fight. I could tell that day you—"

"That day I kicked your ass?" Gaia supplied.

"I think there was mutual ass kicking there, but yeah," Jake said.

"Look, I'm not a joiner," Gaia said as she climbed the front steps of the school. "It's just not me. And I'm not only being selfish here. Trust me. I am not a reliable teammate."

Or a reliable friend, or girlfriend or daughter. . .

"Okay, what's it gonna take to convince you?" Jake

asked, holding open the door for her. Gaia paused for a moment. Well, that was unexpected. Jake didn't seem like the door-opening type. She glanced at his unabashedly hopeful face, then slipped inside.

"What if I do your physics homework for a month?" Jake asked.

"Don't care about homework," Gaia replied, fishing out the second half of her first doughnut.

"What if I. . . get you an excuse note for gym for a month?" Jake offered.

"Like gym," Gaia replied, momentarily wondering how it was he could offer such a thing. She popped a piece of doughnut into her mouth.

"What if I. . ." Jake stopped in the middle of the crowded hallway to think. Gaia kept walking.

"What if I buy you Dunkin' Donuts every morning for a month?" Jake called out, his tone pleading yet confident. She was glad her back was to him so he couldn't see the sudden smile that lit her face. There it was again—that skitter of excitement.

Damn, Gaia thought. *Jake Montone? I'm having. . .* feelings *about Jake Montone?*

He was so the opposite of the guys she liked. So the opposite of Sam and his laid-back, unconscious sexiness. So the opposite of Ed and his self-deprecating humor and kindness. Jake was a guy's guy. He was confident and cocky and strong. In short, he was the kind of guy Gaia liked to take down a few pegs. But still, there was something different about Jake. Something that was causing these skitters. And if she was going to be perfectly honest with herself, those skitters were something she wouldn't mind feeling more often. It wasn't like there were many pleasant emotions to be had these days.

Gaia took a deep breath, her mouth full.

Don't do it, don't do it, don't do it, a little voice in her head chided.

But there were other reasons to say yes. The guy was offering a free month's worth of chocolaty goodness. Plus she'd get to kick the crap out of all those annoying guys on the team. Plus, skitters or no, Jake was pretty much the only person outside of Oliver who was interested in talking to her.

But she couldn't go to practices and meets right now. She had to focus on finding Tatiana and on finding her father.

"Gaia?" Jake said.

Then it hit her. The factor helped the pros edge out any cons. Jake and Tatiana. They'd been getting kind of buddy-buddy there before Tatiana had gone all psycho assassin on her. And he was friends with all the people who Tatiana was *really* close with. People who Tatiana might have confided in or at least slipped up in front of. Jake could be her in.

It was a slim shot, but it was still a shot. And maybe. . . Yes, if she started hanging out with Jake at karate practices, she could also find out what those skitters were all about.

Gaia turned around and looked at Jake, waiting a few yards away. "Okay," she said. "You've got a deal."

Inexplicably Full

JAKE LEANED HIS ELBOWS BACK ON the bleacher seat behind him, watching while Gaia made fairly short work of Erik Chin, arguably the best fighter on the team, after Jake of course. Jake was going for casual and detached, but in truth, he had to concentrate to keep from leaning forward and, well, salivating. He couldn't keep his eyes off Gaia.

She was unbelievable—so focused, so powerful. She looked amazing out there. She looked— he had to admit it—*sexy*. What was *that* about? Up until now Jake had thought there were three requirements for sexy: skin, red lips, and some kind of visible lace. Now all of a sudden he was attracted to a sweaty disheveled girl in huge karate whites who never wore lipstick and was undoubtedly a cotton-undergarments-only type. He really needed to snap out of it.

Gaia sliced her hand across the back of Eric's neck, he fell to his knees, and she elbow-dropped him flat on his face.

"Oh! Ooooh! Augh!" Carlos groaned animatedly next to Jake, wincing and shielding his face from the awful sight. "I can't even look," he said, his left knee pulled up and away from the gym floor and the mat on which the fight was taking place. "Is he still fighting back?"

"He is," Jake replied, absently digging his thumbnail under the nail on his forefinger.

"Poor bastard." Carlos hazarded a glance again. Gaia picked Erik up over her head and tossed him behind her back.

"Is that even legal?" Carlos blurted as the rest of the team squeezed their eyes shut and muttered epithets.

"Not really," Jake replied, his heart pounding.

"So should we stop them?" Carlos asked.

"I'll tell her later," Jake said with a smirk. On top of the serious attraction he was battling, he was also having too much fun watching someone else get their nuts handed to them by Gaia Moore. He'd been the victim of many mockings after the first-day-of-school whupping he'd taken from the girl. Now at least he was no longer alone.

A couple of seconds later Gaia pinned Erik to the mat and held him there for a few moments longer than necessary. Erik's whole body was limp. It was clear to Jake that he wasn't even going to try to get up. He looked over at the bleachers, his eyes begging someone to just call the match already.

"Okay!" Jake said, sitting up straight and resting his forearms on his knees. It was a relief to release his kicked-back pose. "You can let him go now, G.," he said.

Gaia glanced up, her expression almost surprised, as if she'd just been yanked from a deep sleep. Jake's heart skipped a beat and he smiled. He knew the feeling. Whenever he got a good fight going, it felt like he was functioning on some other plane—a plane where he was completely focused, channeling all his power and energy into his movements. Coming down from that feeling was always a letdown.

Gaia released Erik and scrambled up. The karate uniform Jake had lent her puffed out around the belt comically and the legs had come unrolled, so that her feet were completely hidden in the white folds. Jake tried not to smile, but it was hard. She looked like a little girl who'd borrowed Daddy's pajamas. Large clumps of hair hung limply around her reddened face, loosened from her ponytail. She'd broken a bit of a sweat, and it made her skin shine under the fluorescent lights of the gym.

Erik staggered up and stepped to the middle of the mat, where he and Gaia bowed to each other. Then Erik reached out and grasped her hand, shaking his head in amazement.

"I've fought some of the best guys in this city, and I've never had a fight like that," Erik said with an impressed frown.

Gaia's smile lit up the entire room, and Jake's heart responded with another thump. But as quickly as the smile had come it was wiped away again, as if she'd caught herself doing something she wasn't allowed to do and had corrected it as quickly as possible. She cleared her throat as Erik walked back to the bleachers and looked up at Jake expectantly.

"Anyone else?" she asked.

Jake didn't even know what she was talking about. The words didn't penetrate his brain. All he could see was that glistening skin. That glow in her eyes. The little notch in her shoulder that was exposed where his uniform—*his* uniform—slipped slightly to the left. His throat, his heart, his entire chest suddenly felt `inexplicably full`.

There would be no more denying it. He was `falling` for Gaia Moore.

"Jake?" Gaia prompted.

"Uh. . . somebody fight the girl, would ya?"

He was relieved when Greg Marshall finally got up and started to stretch. At least the attention was taken off him as the rest of the guys started to place bets on how long Greg might last.

Now that Jake knew what he wanted, he had to figure out what he was going to do next. Because Jake

Montone was not the type of guy who ignored his urges and desires, who let them fester and stood on the sidelines and hoped and dreamed and fantasized. Once Jake knew what he wanted, he went after it, and usually he got it.

But Gaia Moore was an unusual case—a rare breed. This one would have to be approached with the utmost care. Jake smiled to himself as he watched her toss Greg Marshall over her shoulder like a salad. A protective athletic cup would probably be a good idea as well.

Mr. Elephant Stench

"LOOK, I'M NOT GENERALLY IN THE habit of. . . you know. . . wasting my time," Brendan said in his thick Brooklyn accent. The thug Tatiana's new bartender friend had hooked her up with had turned out to have a goatee, a serious leather fetish, and a gang of buddies who he claimed were willing to do anything she asked. . . for the right price. Patience, however, was not one of his virtues. He glanced at his big silver watch and then shook his arm until the timepiece disappeared under the cuff of his black leather jacket once again.

As she stood waiting for Gaia to leave the school building, Tatiana attempted a patient smile and bit back the retort on the tip of her tongue. Apparently he wasn't in the habit of bathing, either—something that she had become acutely aware of in the hour and a half they'd been standing together, waiting for Gaia to make an appearance. Of all the things that her acquaintance with Gaia had forced her to do over the last three months, this little olfactory nightmare was the one that Tatiana would be least likely to forgive. "Just give it a few more minutes, okay?" Tatiana said in her sweetest voice, fluttering her eyelashes. "If you're going to do a job, you might as well do it right."

She laid her hand gently on his broad chest and trailed it down toward his waist slowly. Predictably, Brendan leered at her, showing the gap between his two front teeth, then returned his attention to the school.

If I ever actually have to kiss that, I'm definitely going to throw up, Tatiana thought. She sighed and rested her chin on her hand on top of the parking meter in front of her, training her eyes on the big metal doors across the way. Could she possibly have missed Gaia's exit? Did she ever take another way out of the school? Over the past few months Tatiana's most important assignment had been to learn each and every one of Gaia's habits. If she had some other mode of escape from the Village School, Tatiana didn't know about it, and that basically made her the worst spy of all time.

Suddenly the doors flew open and out walked Gaia with Jake Montone at her heels. Tatiana ducked down slightly while letting out a small sigh of relief. They both looked flushed and slightly sweaty, as if they'd just gotten out of gym class, but Tatiana happened to know that they had gym sixth period, which was over three hours ago.

"That's her," Tatiana said, even as her brain rushed ahead, searching for a possible explanation for Gaia's and Jake's disheveled appearance.

Tatiana bit her lip. They couldn't have been. . . fooling around in there, could they? That would certainly explain the fact that their clothes had that just-thrown-on look and that they kept glancing at each other uncertainly, almost furtively. Their heads were bent closer together than was necessary, and Tatiana was almost certain she actually saw Gaia smile.

An unexpected twist of jealousy bored through Tatiana's heart. Here she was, on the lam, in hiding with Mr. Elephant Stench, and Gaia had spent her afternoon rolling around in the reference section of the library with that hot piece of Italian ass. Could this situation be any more unfair?

"That girl?" Brendan said, pointing ever so conspicuously. "It's too easy."

"Don't underestimate her," Tatiana said under her

breath, grabbing his hand and pulling it down. "She's full of surprises."

Jake laughed as he and Gaia rounded a corner, and Tatiana saw Gaia look up at him in surprise, with just a hint of pleasure in her eyes. There was definitely something going on between those two. Most likely, they were too moronic to notice it yet, but Tatiana knew, and that was all that mattered. Now she had her in. She wasn't close with Jake by any means, but Tatiana was an expert at reading people, and she'd hung out with him enough to know how to play him. Jake was definitely a knight-in-shining-armor type. The kind that loved to help, to be the better man, to be honorable, if only to pump his own manly-man ego. If Tatiana could just get him to believe that she was a damsel in distress, he was all hers.

"Well, Natalie," Brendan said, using the fake name she'd given herself, "this little job should not be a problem."

"Like I said, don't be so sure," Tatiana warned, turning her full attention to Brendan now that Gaia was out of sight. "She's an expert fighter, and when you kick her ass, I want it thoroughly kicked." She stood up straight and adjusted the strap of her shoulder bag; then she looked him up and down quickly. He was big, but she had a feeling he was clumsy as well.

"You'd better bring a few friends," she said.

I've always been careful when it comes to girls. I don't get why people go out and date whoever just to date. I don't get guys who go out with girls just to fool around even if the girl has no brain and no interests and no per-sonality. Those are the kind of guys that give the rest of us a bad name—that rep that all we care about is sex and seeing how far we can get a girl to go.

I'm into girls who have minds of their own. The kind of girl who has her own hobbies and her own friends and her own things she's into doing. I'm into girls who are smart and can have real conversations, whether they're about school or politics or foot-ball or movies or even fashion. As long as she has opinions about something, that's what matters. I like a girl who can challenge me, who isn't always there when I call, who has her own life. I like a girl who won't take shit from anyone and who never backs

down from an argument. I like a
girl who's strong.

That's the word, I guess.
Strong.

I've gone out with a couple of
girls who came close to my ideal,
but those relationships didn't
work out. They just sort of fiz-
zled and died. I don't know if it
was me or them, but it just
didn't work.

But I've got to say, I've
never gone out with a girl who
embodied all of these things and
could also kick my ass. Could be
interesting.

Jake was
looking right
through her
carefully
woven
exterior **so**
intoxicating
directly into
her emotions,
and she didn't
even mind.

"THIS CAN'T BE RIGHT. . . . THIS

Permanent Fatal Error

can't be happening!" A hot sheen of perspiration covered Oliver's forehead, and he used an old, graying handkerchief to wipe it away. He was still weak, and his fruitless search was only making him feel weaker.

The computer screen cast the only light in the small, cold office on the top floor of his Brooklyn brownstone. He didn't want the place to appear inhabited to the outside world. But the strain on his eyes had started up a headache hours earlier, and the longer he sat and stared at the glowing screen, the more his temples throbbed. He pulled up the collar on his thick wool sweater to cover his bare neck and shoved his dry, frigid hands under his arms.

The speakers let out another low beep and Oliver's heart leapt hopefully. Maybe this time. He hit the open-mail icon, and a list of new messages popped up in front of him. Five new messages. All of them errors. *Address unknown. . . permanent fatal error. . .*

Oliver pushed the heels of his hands into his eyes, watching the purple-and-red swirls caused by the pressure behind his eyelids. Where had all of Loki's operatives disappeared to? Oliver was sure he had their e-mail handles right. Each and every one of them should have been sitting at their terminals or carrying their BlackBerrys, awaiting his return. No. *Loki's* return.

Had they all just defected in the short time that Loki was away? Were his men so disloyal?

Whereas Loki might have felt angered by this flagrant lack of response, Oliver was still feeling relatively optimistic—he'd only just begun his search, and there were many stones still left unturned. And whereas Loki might have felt the need for a release to alleviate his stress, Oliver felt perfectly peaceful. Whereas Loki might have taken the coffee cup that was delicately perched on the saucer in front of him and thrown it across the room, Oliver gently lifted the cup to his mouth and calmly took a sip.

Just keep searching and eventually something will turn up, he told himself.

But with each passing moment Oliver was becoming increasingly more aware of how Loki might have reacted, and this gave him pause. It was only an awareness at this point, but it was an awareness that frightened him. As if any reminder of the old Loki behavior could incite temptation. As if Oliver could slip back into Loki at any time.

Even though he had awoken from his coma as Oliver Moore—a good person, a person who loved his country and his family, a person who would never hurt a fly unless he was forced—the atrocities he had committed as Loki were all slowly but surely coming back to him. Every person he'd killed and tortured, all the hurt he'd caused Gaia and Tom. Oliver had a good soul, but he also had the vivid memories of doing the most evil things possible, and in spite of all his remorse those memories made him feel powerful. And he liked that feeling. It was a feeling so intoxicating, it was difficult to resist.

But he had no choice. No choice but to resist.

All Oliver could do to get past those intense feelings was to focus. "Think of Gaia and Tom," he said quietly, his slow breaths starting to work their magic on his racing pulse. His fantasy of throwing the coffee cup across the room or causing any more damage was quelled. He opened his eyes and got back to work. He deleted the error messages and started typing e-mails to the next ten operatives on his mental list. Helping Gaia and Tom, if he was still alive, was the only way he could make up for everything Loki had done. And he would make up for it.

No matter what it took.

"YOU HAVE TO COME OVER FOR DINner to celebrate," Jake said, walking backward up Fifth Avenue and causing all the other pedestrians to sidestep around him.

"Celebrate what?" Gaia asked, with the trace of a smile. Ever since

Tomato, Garlic, and Basi

Jake had gotten on the mat at practice and pinned three guys in a row, he'd been exuding the bouncy energy of a five-year-old just released from a day in boring kindergarten. His green eyes were bright, he was sporting a constant grin, and there was a definite spring in his step.

"Celebrate the fact that we are going to make Central beg for mercy at that meet tomorrow!" Jake countered.

"We'll see," Gaia replied, pausing at the corner of Fourteenth to wait for the light to change. Rush hour had begun, and the four-lane road was packed with cars weaving in and out, jockeying for position. She didn't want to think about the meet tomorrow. She knew that if she got the slightest lead about either Tatiana or her father before then, there was a good chance that she wouldn't even be there. And then Jake would be little more than the next victim in the long line of people Gaia had let down.

"Come on!" Jake said, bending slightly at the knee. "My dad had the day off, which means early dinner, homemade sauce. . . freshly baked bread. . . mozzarella that melts in your mouth. . . ."

Gaia's stomach grumbled loudly enough to be heard over the rushing traffic. "Your dad cooks?" she asked, raising her eyebrows as the Walk sign lit up.

"My dad *creates*," Jake corrected her, starting across the street. "Don't ever let him hear you reduce it to mere cooking."

Gaia pondered this. She saw herself sitting down

for an actual meal at an actual table. Saw herself sitting across from Jake, talking, maybe even laughing.

You need to get a clue, Gaia told herself, wanting to laugh over the datelike quality the scenario in her head had taken on. *He's offering you food, not some kind of dear-diary moment.*

Which was good, considering she was not looking for a date and she would never keep a diary if her life depended on it.

"Say yes," Jake said with a grin. "You won't regret it, I swear."

"Okay, I'm in," Gaia said, trying to ignore the little flip her heart did over his smile.

"Cool. My dad loves company," Jake said, turning down Fifteenth Street.

Gaia followed, wondering why it was that Jake was only mentioning his father. *My dad had the day off. . . . My dad loves company. . . .* But she knew better than to pry. Jake's family life was none of her business. Besides, once you started asking a person about his life, he started asking you about yours, and she definitely didn't want to go there.

Jake walked over to the glass doors of a swank-looking gray brick building, and the doorman jumped to welcome them.

"Evening, Mr. Montone," the white-haired man said with a nod as he held open the door. "Miss," he said, smiling kindly at Gaia.

"Evening, Rick," Jake said.

They crossed a hushed, intricately tiled lobby to an elevator with mirrored doors. It opened the moment Jake pressed the button and ascended soundlessly to the seventeenth floor. Gaia was accosted by the vision of her ratty reflection in the foggy silver walls of the elevator. She made an attempt at smoothing down her hair and tried to straighten her clothes a bit. Jake's father might be a `company-lover`, but she didn't want him to think his son had picked her up off the street.

Unfortunately, there wasn't much she could do with herself before the elevator doors slid open again. She was just going to have to hope the man was blind or something.

As she and Jake got out of the elevator, Gaia's mouth started to water like Pavlov's dog at the heady scent that permeated the hallway. Nothing like the smell of `tomato, garlic, and basil` to get your appetite going.

"That's him," Jake said referring to the aromatic extravaganza created by his father. Jake pulled a large clump of keys out of his pocket and opened the door to apartment 17A.

"Dad! We're home!" Jake called out.

The scents were even more intense inside, and Gaia suddenly felt weak with hunger. Jake led her into a large, comfortably decorated living room/dining room, where the table was already set for two. He tossed his book bag and jacket onto the couch, and Gaia shrugged off her things. Jake took them from her and laid them out neatly across an armchair. Gaia stifled a smile. If he knew what her stuff had been through, he wouldn't have been so reverent about it.

"Who's 'we'?" a cheery male voice called out. It was followed by the appearance of Jake's father himself, a tall, stocky man with a bit of a belly, who emerged from the kitchen, wiping his hands on a half apron. His hair was black but peppered with gray and receding at the temples. He looked at Gaia and grinned the most welcoming grin she'd ever been graced with.

"Hello!" he said.

"Hey," Gaia replied, feeling suddenly shy. Why was it she could banter for days with evil thugs, but she went tongue-tied in the face of congeniality?

Allergic to nice. . .

"Dad, this is Gaia Moore. Gaia, Arturo Montone, M.D.," Jake said.

"Nice to meet you, Gaia!" the man said, shaking her hand. "You're a friend of Jake's from school?"

"Yeah," Jake replied. "She just joined the karate team."

"Ah. . . a fighter!" Jake's father said, impressed. "I like a girl who can take of herself."

"Uh. . . thanks," Gaia said, feeling it was her turn to speak.

"Well, I'll grill you more over dinner," Jake's father said with a wink.

Great, Gaia thought sarcastically.

"He's kidding," Jake said.

Dr. Montone smiled as Gaia let out a breath. She wasn't used to so much positive energy bombarding her like this.

"You sit," Dr. Montone told her, unexpectedly reaching out to touch her arm. "Jake, get her a place setting! Dinner's almost ready."

He bustled back into the kitchen, and Jake pulled out a chair at the gleaming redwood table. Gaia stood there as Jake walked over to a hutch and removed a plate, a set of silverware, and a place mat. When he turned around again, he stopped in his tracks.

"That chair's for you, you know," he said, glancing at the seat he'd pulled out.

Gaia flushed, feeling like a moron, and sat down hard. How stupid was she? Did she think he'd pulled out the chair for fun? Because of some kind of weird OCD complex? Of course it was for her.

As Jake set the place in front of Gaia, she suddenly became hyperaware of her hands. She didn't know where to put them. They went from the table to her lap to the arms of her chair and finally back to the table, where she folded them together awkwardly.

Searching for something to focus on to help her stop obsessing about her total discomfort, Gaia's eyes fell on a framed photograph on the countertop of the hutch. The woman in the picture was gorgeous—raven haired with huge blue eyes and a flirtatious smile that was the mirror image of Jake's. Gaia knew she was looking at Jake's mother and wondered again where she was. The woman's gaze was mesmerizing, and Gaia couldn't seem to take her eyes off her. But she suddenly felt Jake hovering behind her chair, ready to put down a drinking glass.

"Sorry," Gaia muttered, reddening. Why had she agreed to this? She should be scarfing down a dirty-water dog right now on the train back to Brooklyn. Gaia wasn't accustomed to being waited on.

"That's my mom," Jake said as he placed the glass down a little too hard.

"She's. . . really. . ." *Really what, Gaia? Is it really so difficult to think of something nice to say?*

"I know," Jake interrupted, walking around the table and sitting across from Gaia. "She was really beautiful."

"Was?" Gaia asked before she could rethink it.

Jake cleared his throat and looked down at his empty plate as his father clanged around in the kitchen. "She died when I was ten years old," he said. "Brain tumor."

Gaia's heart went cold. He had said it so simply, but there was so much pain and emotion wrapped up in that statement. And Gaia knew all of it. She knew the anger he probably felt toward his mother for deserting him. She knew the guilt he probably felt over that anger. She knew how he would probably give up his life for one more day with her.

"I'm sorry," she said. "I didn't mean to—"

"It's all right," Jake said, an edge in his voice.

Gaia stared into his light eyes, which were suddenly filled with defiance. She knew that feeling. He was daring her to be sympathetic—daring her to pity him. Oh, how she hated it when people gave her those sorry-ass looks when they heard about her own mother.

"What about you?" Jake asked suddenly, crossing his arms over his chest. "What's your family like?"

There it was. Ask a person a question and it comes right back to bite you in the ass.

I don't think I can answer that one without a graph and a couple of pie charts, Gaia thought, swallowing hard. But Jake was watching her expectantly. She had to say *something.*

"My mom died when I was little, too," Gaia offered, hoping that sharing this one piece of information might at least take that sorrowful-yet-hard look out of Jake's eyes.

"Really?" Jake asked. "How?"

"It was an accident," Gaia replied quickly. Now it was her turn to become entranced by her plate.

"You know what sucks?" Jake said.

This conversation? Gaia thought. "What?"

"The fact that everyone always says they understand

how you feel about it but they never can," Jake said. "No one ever can."

Gaia's heart pounded painfully in her chest, and she looked up into Jake's eyes. In that one moment there was a connection that even Gaia couldn't deny. She knew something about him that no one else could come close to knowing and he about her. And the really strange thing was, it didn't bother her. It was as if Jake was looking right through her carefully woven exterior directly into her emotions, and she didn't even mind. She actually felt kind of. . . free.

"Exactly," Gaia said quietly. "I know exactly what you mean."

"HEY, RED! LOOKIN' HOT!"

Tatiana tilted her head to the side so that the red curls fell between her face and the Neanderthal who was catcalling to her from the doorway to the twenty-four-hour Dunkin' Donuts around the corner from the Village School. This whole wig thing was turning out to be an interesting sociological experiment. That was the third guy who'd come on to her since she'd left the safe house twenty minutes ago. Maybe blonds had more fun, but redheads definitely attracted more moronic come-ons.

She rounded the corner, grabbed the red curls on either side of her head, and yanked down on the wig, fitting it more snugly against her skull. It was dark out now, and if anyone saw her approaching the school, there was no way they would recognize her with the mass of hair shielding her face. Still, she wanted to get this over and done with.

The front door was always unlocked, even this late, so that overachieving teachers could come and go. The janitors were also at work inside somewhere, but Tatiana was sure very few people were left. It was her only chance to get in and out undetected.

She opened and closed the heavy metal door as quietly as possible, producing only a tiny click as it shut. She crept up the stairs and peeked around the corner to the main hall, left, then right. Every other fluorescent light was illuminated, casting an eerie glow over the deserted hallway. Tatiana took a deep breath and walked quickly, silently to the stairwell.

When she opened the door to the second floor, she heard movement and hushed voices to her left and paused. Damn kiss-ass teachers. How much money could they possibly be getting paid? Certainly not enough to keep them here this late. She trained her ear on the sounds and relaxed. They were definitely coming from the front hall—the opposite direction of where she had to go. She slipped out of the stairwell and slid along the wall this time, ready to duck into a classroom if anyone happened to decide on a bathroom run.

Jake's locker was at the end of a row, directly across from another stairwell. Tatiana pulled the folded note out of her jacket pocket and shoved it into one of the three chevron-shaped slats in the door, wondering if they'd been expressly designed to accept secret admirer cards and Dear John letters. She heard the paper flutter to the floor inside and turned to go, mission accomplished.

But just as she was registering the fact that she was home free, she heard footsteps running up the stairs right in front of her. Suddenly Megan appeared beyond the cut-glass window in the wooden door, her face downturned as she dug in her backpack, looking for something. Tatiana had nowhere to hide. She had only seconds to think. She whipped off her wig and smiled. At that moment Megan opened the door and looked up.

"Omigod!" she blurted, jumping back against the door and bringing her hand over her heart. Her moment of surprise gave Tatiana a chance to stuff the wig into her pocket. "Tatiana! You scared me!"

"Sorry," Tatiana said. "I guess this place *is* kind of deserted. What are you doing here?" *Besides completely screwing me over?* she added silently.

"Oh, the spirit club meeting went late," Megan explained with a smile. She resumed the search of her backpack. "We were making signs and stuff for the karate meet tomorrow." Finally Megan pulled out a tube of lip balm and quickly applied it to her lips, then smacked them together. "You know, when Tara came up with this whole idea of equal opportunity pep, I was all for it, but keeping up with all these teams and their meets gets kind of exhausting."

"I know," Tatiana said sympathetically. "Well, I'd better get going...."

"What are *you* doing here?" Megan asked, tossing her hair over her shoulder and completely ignoring Tatiana's attempt to bail. Two little lines appeared just above her nose, rendering her the picture of concern. "You haven't been in school for a couple of days."

"Yeah. . . there's been some family stuff going on," Tatiana said, knowing Megan would eat up the idea of being let in on a private drama. "I'd rather not talk about it."

Megan raised her eyebrows. "Oh, I totally understand," she said. "But. . . why are you here, then?"

There is nothing worse than a girl with a nose for gossip, Tatiana thought.

"I came to get some stuff out of my locker," Tatiana lied easily, tilting her head to indicate the locker just behind her. "I want to keep up with my homework."

Megan's face scrunched up in confusion. "That's Jake Montone's locker," she said. "Yours is downstairs."

Tatiana had to concentrate to keep from rolling her

eyes. Of course. How could she have forgotten the many times that Megan had tracked her down at her locker to chat and giggle and exchange lipsticks? Not only that, but Megan was completely obsessed with Jake. She probably knew not only where his locker was, but his combination, his favorite food in the cafeteria, and the number of freckles on his arms.

"Okay, you caught me," Tatiana said, thinking quickly. If Megan kept such a keen eye on Jake, then she would notice when he found the note in the morning, and she was smart enough to put two and two together and realize Tatiana had left it. It was time to tell a version of the truth. "I was leaving a note for Jake."

Megan's eyes lit up with interest. She walked over to a locker a few doors down and started spinning the lock.

"Really?" she said provocatively. "You and Jake Montone, huh?"

"Yeah," Tatiana said, forcing a blush to her cheeks. "But. . . don't tell anyone, okay?" she added. "I mean, I think Gaia sort of has a crush on him and I wouldn't want her to find out that I was here. . . ."

"Please," Megan said. "Like I would really talk to Gaia Moore."

That, at least, was one thing Tatiana had going for her in this whole mess. Megan might love to gossip, but she'd rather wear acid-washed jeans to school than be caught talking to Gaia. And even if she did tell all her friends about the note, the news would never get back to Ms. Moore. No one bothered to let the girl in on anything.

"So. . . have you guys. . . you know. . . ?" Megan said, her interested tone barely masking her jealousy.

Tatiana smiled. There would be no harm in having a little fun with the girl.

"I will say that the boy is not shy," Tatiana said with a loaded grin. "And that whole phrase about the size of a guy's shoe. . . ? Totally true."

Megan groaned and blushed the color of Tatiana's hidden wig. "You're so bad!" she said.

You have no idea, Tatiana thought. "See you around," she said, fluttering her fingers at Megan. Then she turned and strode out of the school, hoping the girl would, for once, keep her big mouth shut.

How could I have been so careless? If my mother could see what I have done in the past few days, she would be in shock. I am not acting like the daughter she taught so well. I am not following procedure. I should have made sure there was no one left in the school to catch me. I should never have taken that car on the street. But I know why I have become this way. I know why I keep stepping away from protocol.

I have to save my mother. And I am letting my emotions cloud my judgment. It only makes it worse that Gaia is involved. More emotions. More clouds.

I must take a step back and make sure I do not make any more errors. I must go over every inch of my plan and strengthen the weak links. Because this is one mission I cannot afford to lose.

I am my mother's daughter, and I have to start thinking like her. If our positions were reversed and I was the one who was taken, she would have found me by now. She would not have let anyone or anything stand in her way. Gaia would have talked, and she would be lying dead right now with a bullet between her eyes. My mother and I would be together.

And that is all I want. I want us to be together, and I want Gaia dead. Jake is my only hope. I have to play this just right. And I will. I will play it like my mother would play it. I will be cold, I will be smart, I will be ruthless. I will be her.

And I will win. I must.

From: X22

To: Y

Subject: URGENT!

Our techs have picked up heavy activity from the private account of subject L. Subject L has been reactivated. Situation needs immediate attention. How is this possible? Please advise.

From: Y

To: X22

Subject: Re: URGENT!

This is not possible. Subject L has not been reactivated. Unknown agent must have broken his password, which we, I remind you, have yet to do. We must locate this agent, get the information, and terminate the agent. I have already assigned B team to the search. In the meantime, continue to monitor account activity.

Repeat: It is not possible that subject L has been reactivated.

How had
everything
impossible
gotten so
complicated?

WHEN GAIA LEFT JAKE'S APARTMENT

over an hour later, she was reveling in the contentment brought on by a good meal. Her stomach was full, her head was clear, and **Epiphany** she was filled with a sudden sense of purpose. Watching Jake and his dad participating in the familial conversation over dinner had left Gaia with an intense need to be around people she cared about. Unfortunately, she'd managed to either alienate or completely lose track of every last one of them. But there was one person she might still be able to make things right with.

She swung a brown bag of leftovers as she pushed open the door of Dmitri's apartment building. It was time to talk to Sam.

He's had a few days to cool off, Gaia reasoned with herself as the elevator zipped skyward. *And he understands what my life is like. He has to understand why my first instinct is always to be suspicious. . . .*

Of course, none of her reasoning could erase the memory of the destroyed expression Sam had worn when she'd accused him of setting her up for an assassination attempt. He had looked as betrayed as she had felt when a hail of gunfire was opened up on her.

Yeah. He may take a little convincing, Gaia thought, hoping for the best as she rang the doorbell. Maybe she could bribe him with Dr. Montone's leftovers.

She heard footsteps, too heavy to be Dmitri's, and held her breath. She could practically *feel* Sam looking through the peephole at her. Hear him breathing. She counted silently while he thought over whether or not he wanted to open the door.

One... two... three... four...

Oh, come on, it can't be that *hard to decide.*

Nine... ten... eleven...

Gaia shifted from foot to foot and felt her body start to grow warm with embarrassment and anger. How could he leave her hanging like this? She felt like a complete and total idiot. Like the dork who went to the hot girl's house to pick up his dream date for the prom, only to find out she had already left with the quarterback and it was all a big joke on him.

Twenty-one... twenty-two...

This was completely uncalled for.

"Sam? I know you're there!" she said finally.

The door opened, causing Gaia's heart to skip an excited beat, and she braced herself for the wary look that was sure to be on Sam's face. But no one was there. She pushed the door until it hit the wall and saw Sam's back retreating toward the living room. She took a deep breath, squared her shoulders, and followed him. This was going to be harder than she thought.

When she got to the living room, Sam was shoving notebooks, pens, and a baseball cap, among other things, into his backpack. Gaia waited for him to acknowledge her. He didn't.

"Sam, look, I—"

"Dmitri's not here," he said, immersed in his frantic, rather violent packing. "He took off this morning. Said he'd be gone for a few days. Something about. . . staying under the radar."

Gaia barely had the wherewithal to assess this statement. She was too busy noticing how much concentration Sam was putting into not looking at her.

"I'm here to talk to you," Gaia said, reddening.

"Well, you'd better come back another time, then, because I'm on my way out," Sam replied. He zipped up his bag and finally looked at her, though his eyes were so hard, she could barely tell if they were focusing on anything at all.

Wow. He wasn't making this easy. The last words she could imagine herself uttering in the face of such coldness were *I'm sorry*. It was pretty clear they were just going to ricochet right off his icy exterior. He started to brush past her, and Gaia reflexively grabbed his shoulder.

"Wait!" she blurted, realizing that if she was going to get out an apology, it would have to be fast. "Sam, I wanted to say. . . I'm sorry."

Okay, that was weird. Usually she had to rev up for a good fifteen minutes before she could actually speak those words.

"Yeah, you told me that already," Sam said flatly, yanking his arm away. She felt like he had slapped her right in the face.

"Sam, you have to try to understand," Gaia told him, the area around her heart roiling with heat and emotion. "I just. . . I never know who I can trust. You know that I—"

"You should have known you could trust me," Sam spat, his eyes still hard. "After everything I've been through for you. . . ." He tipped back his head and groaned. "I am not going to do this," he snapped, his words piercing Gaia's heart. "I've had enough. 'I'm sorry' is just not gonna cut it, Gaia."

"Then what will?" Gaia asked.

Sam took a deep breath and let it out slowly. "I don't know. I don't know if anything ever will."

The huge meal Gaia had eaten started to rebel against her stomach the moment Sam turned his back on her and grabbed his jacket off a coatrack in the corner. She swallowed hard before speaking.

"Where are you going?" she asked.

"Out," he said, pulling on his jacket.

"Sam, I don't know if that's a good idea," Gaia said, trying to ignore the emotion coming off him like a tidal wave. "I mean, you might not. . . be. . . safe. . . ."

She trailed off as she realized that she was actually living with the one and only person who Sam was hiding from. Which meant that she was technically harboring his enemy. But then, he was Oliver, not Loki, so she wasn't really doing anything wrong per se. Gaia shook her head slightly to try to straighten it all out. How had everything gotten so complicated?

"I can't just sit in this apartment for the rest of my life, either," Sam said, his voice full of accusation. The underlying meaning: *"And I wouldn't have to if it wasn't for you."*

Gaia couldn't argue. After all, she knew where his former captor was and what he was doing at this very moment. She was pretty sure he would actually be quite safe out on the streets. She turned away from him and put her things down on the coffee table.

"Okay, so where are you going?" she asked, shoving her hands into the back pockets of her cargo pants.

"I found out there's some guy down in Alphabet City who might be able to get me a copy of my license so I can get access to my bank account and stuff," Sam said. "I can't keep living off of Dmitri. . . ."

Gaia suddenly felt stunned, like she'd just been in a head-on collision and time had stopped and she was just coming to. Everything Sam had said after the words *Alphabet City* was completely lost in the ether.

Alphabet City—the words scrolled across her mind.
AlphaBet City.
AlphaBet City. . . SH.
Alphabet City safe house.

That was it. It had to be. The key she'd found at the

apartment must be the key to a safe house that Natasha had set up in Alphabet City, the semiseedy area downtown east of the Village.

"Gaia? Why the hell are you looking at me like that?" Sam asked suddenly, yanking Gaia out of her mental happy dance.

Gaia snapped her mouth shut. She realized that she hadn't been listening to a word Sam had said. She was too busy having her epiphany. She looked at him, her face aglow with triumph. She could have kissed him for sparking the breakthrough she'd just had, but under the circumstances she was sure a kiss would go over about as well as a solid punch to the gut. Besides, she was anti–spontaneous kissing by nature.

"I have to go," she said, as close to giddy as she'd ever been in her life.

She grabbed up her bags and bustled by a stunned Sam, racing for the door. Sam was not going to forgive her now—from what he'd told her, he might never forgive her. But as much as she wanted him back in her life, she was going to have to deal with that later. Right now she was one step closer to finding Tatiana, and that took her one step closer to finding her dad. Armed with this new information, she had to get back to the Seventy-second Street apartment and make sure there was nothing she had missed.

She scrambled through the doorway and decided to take the stairs.

BY THE TIME GAIA RETURNED TO THE

The Spy Game

brownstone later that night, all traces of her earlier optimism had been swept under the rug, taken out to the trash, and hauled off to a landfill in Staten Island. So what if she figured out what *ABCSH* stood for. What could she do with that information—knock on every apartment door in Alphabet City until Tatiana answered? Still, she forced herself to climb all three flights of stairs to Oliver's office. Maybe he'd have some good news for her to relighten her mood.

"I'm. . . back," Gaia said, trudging into the dark room and falling into the old moldy couch against the wall next to Oliver's desk. He sat hunched over his keyboard, the green glow of the computer screen casting an eerie array of shadows across his face. The tiny square of the screen's reflection danced in his eyes as he scanned the information he'd just brought up.

"This is not going well," he said, focused on the computer.

Gaia's stomach turned. So much for that.

"Nothing, huh?" she asked, slumping farther down in her seat.

"I've been working all day. . . trying to get in touch with Loki's men," he said, finally leaning back.

He let out a sigh and rubbed at his face with both

hands. When he looked at her, he blinked a few times as if he was trying to clear his sight. His eyes were glassy and rimmed with red, and his skin was the color of snow. Gaia looked around the desk and saw that there was nothing. No food wrappers, no glasses or plates—only one single coffee cup.

"Have you been up here all day?" Gaia asked, her brow creasing.

"I haven't moved from in front of this thing," Oliver said seriously. "I haven't even gone to the bathroom."

Okay. That was an overshare, Gaia thought. But still, she was impressed. Oliver was clearly determined to do everything he could to help her find her father. She allowed herself a slight smile. It was nice to have someone on her side. But he wasn't going to be doing anyone any good if he got himself sick through lack of food and. . . lack of bathroom runs.

"Maybe you should take a break."

"I'm not going to stop until I find Tom," Oliver said firmly, looking her in the eye with a suddenly clear and steady gaze. It was a tone that Gaia knew better than to argue with.

"Thank you," she said. "But tomorrow morning I'm going to get you some food."

Oliver smiled. "That would be good," he said. He returned his attention to the computer and leaned his elbows on the table at either side of his keyboard. "I just wish I had more to go on."

Gaia's mind instantly flashed to the key in the small pocket of her messenger bag. She pulled out the envelope and held it out to Oliver, her hand shaking ever so slightly. It was the only connection she had left to Tatiana and her father.

"I found this at our old apartment," Gaia said. "The one I shared with the two women who took my dad."

Oliver glanced at her and then took the envelope gingerly from her fingers. He dumped out the key and turned it over in his palm.

"It's old," he said, tossing it up and catching it. "Heavy."

"Look at what it says on the envelope," Gaia instructed. "I think it stands for Alphabet City safe house."

Oliver frowned at the scrawled letters. "A good assessment," he said. He glanced at her and smiled wanly. "I'd say there's hope for you in the spy game yet."

Gaia returned a wry smile. They both knew that she didn't want anything to do with the spy game, no matter how good she'd proved herself to be. It was outside forces that were always keeping her on the playing board. She let out a long sigh.

"The problem is, my stellar assessment doesn't do us much good," Gaia said, pushing her hands into her hair, then trailing them down her face. "It's not like I can go down there and try every single door in the neighborhood."

"No," Oliver said, clicking on a desk lamp and holding the key up to the light. "But that may not be necessary. With a key like this, there may be ways of narrowing down the door it matches." He slipped the key back into the envelope and placed it on the desk next to his mouse pad. "The Internet has been good for nothing all day, but this may prove to be an easier task," he said, smiling at her again.

Gaia took a deep breath. It was still odd to be in the same room with this man. Whether he was Oliver or Loki, his hands were still the hands that had killed so many people—that had taken loved ones away from her. She knew that no one else could help her, but knowing that didn't stop her from wishing things were different. No matter how hard Oliver worked, no matter how hard he tried to prove himself to her, it was still very hard to trust him. Almost impossible.

Look at him, Gaia told herself as Oliver started to tap away at the keyboard. *He's exhausted and hungry and weak and he still won't stop. That has to count for something.*

She walked over to the far wall, grabbed a dusty, rickety wooden chair, and joined Oliver at the computer. If he was going to be tireless, so was she.

WALKING EAST ON HOUSTON STREET,

Alphabet City

Jake pressed the note between two fingers in the pocket of his denim jacket. His palms were dry, his breath was normal, but his heart was pounding just a little bit faster than usual. He wasn't nervous, just. . . intrigued. This was by no means the first time a girl had left a secret note in his locker, but he had a feeling that this wasn't just any run-of-the-mill "I have a crush on you" meeting. For one thing, Tatiana hadn't been in school for days. For another, he'd had to cut class to make this little rendezvous. And now he was headed to Alphabet City, a neighborhood about as far from the one Tatiana lived in—both literally and socially—as you could get and still be on the island.

Something was up. Jake could feel it.

He turned up Avenue B and spotted the tiny coffee shop, Café Mille Lucci, that Tatiana had described in her note. He approached the pink-tinted window and saw her sitting in a booth, her face partially obscured by the neon Hot Coffee sign that was suspended from the glass in front of him. Huh. She didn't look sick or anything. This was just getting more and more bizarre.

Jake walked in and plopped down in the seat across from Tatiana's. Her face lit up when she saw him as if she hadn't spoken to another living soul in days.

"Jake! You came!" she said with a smile.

"Yeah," he replied. He didn't remove his jacket, and when the waitress approached, he shook his head at her. He didn't want Tatiana to think that he was getting comfortable. "So what's with the cloak-and-dagger? Where have you been the last couple of days?

Megan and all her friends can't stop talking about how worried they are," he added dryly.

It was true that Megan and her little friends hadn't stopped talking about Tatiana for the past two days, but he had a feeling they were less worried and more salivating for a scandal.

"I've just been. . . dealing with some family stuff," Tatiana said, averting her gaze.

Jake got that. And he knew better than to ask questions. Family stuff either meant, "I don't want to talk about it," or, "Ask me and I'll talk for days." He didn't want to offend, and he also didn't want to spend the next hour listening to Tatiana purge. The cleanup of emotional spillage was not his area of expertise.

Although if Gaia *had wanted to spill about her mother, I would have listened,* he realized, almost smiling. But Gaia was another story. Gaia was another *epic.*

"So. . . why am I here?" Jake asked. He didn't want to be blunt, but it wasn't like he and Tatiana were good friends. Sure, he'd hung out with her in a group, but this was the longest mano-a-mano conversation they'd ever had. Maybe she *did* have a crush on him.

"I was wondering if you'd do me a favor," Tatiana said, her eyes unabashedly filled with hope.

"What's that?" Jake asked, lacing his fingers together on the table in a double fist.

"I need to see Gaia," she said. "I was hoping you would help me set up a meeting with her."

Okay, that was unexpected. Jake's face scrunched in confusion. "Don't you guys, like, live together?" he asked.

"Not anymore," Tatiana replied. Jake couldn't put his finger on it, but something changed in her face when she said this. Like it put a bad taste in her mouth to even think about it.

"Well, can't you call her?" Jake asked.

"I can't do that," Tatiana replied.

Jake sighed and rubbed his forehead. He was losing patience with this conversation. If all Tatiana wanted was a favor, why hadn't she just called one of her real friends? Like Megan or one of the girls? Of course, none of those chicks were friendly with Gaia, but neither was Jake. . . at least not until recently.

"What did she do, stain your favorite sweater or something?" Jake asked with a scoff. He'd been around for some major catfights in his time, but never one where the two parties asked someone to set up a meeting. He felt like he was in the middle of some kind of CIA movie. God. Girls could be so dramatic sometimes.

Tatiana's eyes flashed. "This is a little more serious than that," she said. "It's life or death."

Jake's stomach sent up a warning. She sounded fairly serious. "What do you mean, 'life or death'?"

"I can't really explain," Tatiana said, looking down at her lap. She pulled in a shaky breath, and when she looked up again, her eyes were filled with tears.

The hair on the back of Jake's neck stood on end.

Something was really wrong here. Tatiana put her hands on the table, and he saw that her fingers were trembling. Whatever was happening between Tatiana and Gaia, this girl was really scared. Jake felt the sudden urge to protect her—his urge to be the hero kicking in.

"But Gaia can help you?" Jake asked.

"She's the only one who can," Tatiana answered, one tear spilling over.

"So what do you want me to do?" Jake asked.

"Just set up a meeting between the two of you and tell me where so that I can show up," she said, leaning forward and looking him dead in the eye.

Jake froze. Suddenly his protective instincts were shattered and replaced by nothing but suspicion. Tatiana was still teary, but there was something else in her eyes. Something. . . fierce. What the hell was he getting himself into here?

"No way," he said, sitting back in his vinyl seat, which let out a little hiss. He definitely didn't like the idea of setting Gaia up. Not when he had less than one clue as to what Tatiana was after. "I can't help you unless you tell me exactly what's going on."

Tatiana's back straightened, and Jake was reminded of the way his old cat used to arch her back when threatened. She had the same sort of battle-ready look about her.

"I can't do that," Tatiana said.

Jake stood up and hovered for a moment at the

end of the table. "Well, how 'bout you contact me when you can?" he said. He headed for the door but paused when he heard Tatiana's voice.

"If you change your mind, you can look for me in the evenings here," she said.

Jake rolled his eyes and walked out of the tiny café without a backward glance.

Outside, Jake turned his footsteps toward school and realized his hair was still on end and the he had goose bumps down his arms. Suddenly he was very worried for Gaia. There was something about that Tatiana girl he didn't trust. Something he couldn't quite put his finger on.

Whatever was going on between those two girls, Jake didn't want to get in the middle of it.

When I was young, my mother used to read the classics to me at bedtime. I used to drift off listening to the melody of her comforting voice as she read the Russian translations of books like *The Wizard of Oz, Alice's Adventures in Wonderland,* and *The Story of Doctor Dolittle.* Then one night she tried to read to me from her favorite book, *The Secret Garden,* but after she read the first few chapters to me, I started to cry. I was inconsolable. My mother thought I was just overtired and put me to bed. She tried again the following night.

But when I saw the book the next night, I started to cry again. I wouldn't let her read it. I took it from her hands and threw it across the room. My mother didn't understand what was wrong with me. She held me until I stopped crying, then pushed my hair away from my face and smiled down at me.

"What is wrong, little one?"

she asked me. "Why the tears?"

I told her that I thought it was a horrible book and that I didn't want to hear any more. I asked her to read me anything but that. I would even sit through *Little Women* again, which I hated, if she would promise never to read *The Secret Garden* again.

My mother was confused. Why did I hate the book she loved so much?

"Her mother and father died and left her all alone in that house in India!" I told her, unable to believe that she didn't understand how horrible this was. "No one even cared about her or came looking for her. She was all alone!"

My mother laughed and hugged me and promised me that the story got happier after that. That it was full of hope and life. But I couldn't get the image out of my head. What if my mother died and left me all alone? There would be no one left to care about me. No one would ever find me.

So my mother put the book back
on the shelf and started another.
And she promised me that she
would never leave me alone.
Never. She would always be there
to take care of me.

But now the tables have
turned. Now it's me who needs to
take care of her.

the sudden
flip her
heart
executed **victory**
when
Jake **hug**
tightened
his grasp
on her

COMING OUT OF THE BATHROOM STALL

In the Know

between sixth and seventh period, Gaia caught a glimpse of herself in the aging, scratched mirror that ran the length of the wall across the way. Dark circles had appeared under her eyes, her lips were chapped, and her skin was so pasty, she could have passed for a bottle of Elmer's. She sighed and put her bag down on the metal counter beneath the mirror. For once, though, her hair wasn't in knots.

Exhausted from the all-night Internet search, which had, at least, unearthed a few people in the lock-and-key trade who might be able to help her and Oliver, Gaia had spent the whole school day in a daze. This afternoon she was supposed to fight in that karate match, and she knew Jake was counting on her to help the team win. At this point she just hoped she didn't crawl onto the mat and pass out.

Gaia dug in her bag for some Chapstick, and the door to the bathroom swung open with a loud creak. She didn't look up until she realized that whoever had walked in was standing a few feet away, glaring at her. Gaia's eyes fell on a pair of three-inch-heeled black leather boots and she sighed. It was definitely an FOH.

Let the verbal diarrhea begin.

"So, Gaia, I have a question for you," she said. It was Megan. Gaia glanced at her, then continued her Chapstick search.

This should be good, she thought.

"What the heck did you do to Tatiana?" Megan asked, taking a few clicking steps toward Gaia. "I saw her last night, and she was *not* acting like herself."

Gaia lifted her face. Megan now had her full and undivided attention.

"You saw her last night?" she asked, pulling her bag off the counter and draping it over her shoulder, painful lips forgotten. "Where? When?"

"Here. Around seven," Megan replied, crossing her arms under her Miracle Bra-ed chest. "So why is it that everyone who gets involved with you drops off the face of the earth, huh? Sam Moon. . . Heather Gannis. . . now Tatiana. . ."

Heather hadn't dropped off the face of the earth, but now was not the time to argue semantics with this fairly brainless specimen. It made no sense— Tatiana lurking around school at an hour when she knew Gaia wouldn't be there. Unless she was planting something. Like a bomb, for example. But no. Tatiana would never be that careless. She would never do something that would attract so much attention. Not when she could take Gaia out quickly and quietly by simply following her after school. So what was the point? Gaia needed answers.

"What was she doing here?" she asked.

A slow, knowing smile spread over Megan's lips and she turned to the mirror, leaning in and turning her face from side to side, scrutinizing her perfect makeup.

"I promised her I wouldn't tell," she said, smirking.

Her eyes were dancing with the knowledge that she had information Gaia wanted. And Gaia was sure she was going to let it out. A person like Megan lived to let others know exactly how in the know she was. Gaia crossed her arms over her stomach and waited, eyebrows arched. This was the moment she'd been waiting for—the moment that one of Tatiana's so-called friends would slip up and expose her. But Gaia wouldn't give the twerp the satisfaction of begging for gossip.

Megan looked at Gaia out of the corner of her eye, then swung her blond hair behind her shoulders and turned to face her.

"All right, if you *must* know," she said, as if Gaia had been interrogating her, "she was leaving a note for Jake Montone."

She smiled and watched Gaia carefully, waiting for some kind of reaction. But Gaia was nothing if not good at masking her emotions—in this case shock, glee, and disappointment all rolled into one. A note for Jake. So he *did* know something. It seemed Gaia had chosen the right person to get close to in order to find Tatiana. A small victory.

Still, part of Gaia couldn't help wishing that Jake wasn't, in fact, involved. Part of Gaia just wanted him to be her friend. No espionage attached.

But there was no point in wishing for that now. Jake *was* involved, thanks to Tatiana. And Gaia knew what she had to do.

"Oh, don't feel bad, Gaia," Megan said with false sweetness. "You didn't really think that a guy like Jake would go for a hygienically challenged person like yourself, did you?"

But Gaia didn't even register the insult. She was too busy scanning her brain to see if she knew what class Jake had next. She brushed by Megan and out the door into the thinning crowd in the hallway. Damn. The bell was about to ring. It would have to wait.

But luckily, thanks to Jake himself, she would have plenty of time to pick his brain that afternoon at the karate match. Gaia smiled. Her fingers and toes were tingling with excitement over this latest lead, but she could squelch it for a couple of hours. This afternoon Jake was all hers. Maybe being a joiner wasn't such a bad idea after all.

"POINT! BLUE!" THE REF SHOUTED, thrusting his arm in Gaia's direction from the edge of the mat. The crowd in the bleachers cheered and applauded, and Gaia heard Jake's voice above the rest, shouting, "Yeah! That's it! Finish him off!"

Too Eas

The rest of the team was sitting on the bottom riser, but Gaia could see Jake from the corner of her eye, standing in front of the others, completely focused.

Gaia waited in a fighting stance, feet spread apart, knees bent, hands fisted. She watched her opponent drag himself up off the ground. He was sweating, he was bleeding from the lip, he was gasping for breath. Gaia coolly blew a shock of hair away from her eyes. This really was too easy.

Most of the people Gaia fought had a lot more heart than this guy. Or a lot more desperation, more likely. Or just a lot more evil in their blood. Whatever the case, the difference between the street thugs and drug dealers and Loki operatives she'd fought in the past and this guy with his cropped hair and square jaw was clear. All those other people were fighting for a real reason—survival, revenge, loyalty. This guy was probably fighting because his girlfriend was in the stands somewhere, waiting for him to prove his manhood. Wasn't gonna happen.

"Finish him off!" Jake shouted again.

That was another new thing for Gaia. She couldn't remember the last time she'd had a cheering section for a fight. Her opponent approached her tentatively, his brown eyes begging her to just finish this already. Pathetic. But she could oblige. She was deathly bored.

He made a move to punch, and Gaia lifted her leg and kicked him clean in the jaw, not very hard. He fell on his ass, and the crowd went crazy.

"Point, blue! Match, blue!" the ref shouted, lifting Gaia's arm in the air.

Gaia grinned as her gaze fell on Megan and her pep squad, who cheered her victory, although with less enthusiasm than they had for Jake's win. Then her eyes traveled left and she saw Ed sitting there, clapping grimly. A cute Asian girl sat to his right, cheering and nudging him with her shoulder, trying to get his attention. But Ed didn't even flinch. His eyes were fixed on Gaia.

Her heart twisted painfully, and the smile fell from her face. The girl clearly had a crush on Ed, but he probably had no idea. Ed was clueless when it came to his own attractiveness. And the way he was looking at her. . . She couldn't tell if he hated her or was dying for her to acknowledge him. But it didn't matter. Ed was not going to be in her life. Not anymore.

She tore her eyes away and watched her teammates as they streamed over to her, gleefully whooping and clapping. Her win had also won them the meet, a meet that had been back and forth all afternoon. All she wanted in the world at that moment was to see Ed smile again—to see him happy—but there was nothing she could do about that at this very moment. She wasn't sure there was anything she could do about that at all. She had never made anyone happy in her life.

"That was amazing!" Jake shouted as he rushed over to her.

Gaia's eyes widened in surprise as he grabbed her up in his arms and spun her around in a victory hug. The contact itself was unexpected, but so was the sudden flip her heart executed when Jake tightened his grasp on her. She laughed against her own will, looking down at the smiling faces of her new teammates. For once she was a true celebrated hero. Maybe the victory was a silly one, but it felt good nonetheless.

Jake replaced her on the ground, and his smiling face was just inches from her own. But the second she looked into his eyes again, she remembered. This guy was getting secret notes from Tatiana. He might even know where the girl was hiding. This was no time to dwell on heart flips or on the thrill of victory or on the fact that Ed was stalking out of the gym right now, Asian girl in tow.

"We should go out and celebrate," Jake said.

"I'm in," Gaia replied, not missing a beat.

If Jake knew anything, she was going to find out what it was. And she was going to find out today.

Internal Warning System

"SO. . . SOLID FIGHT," JAKE SAID, taking two ice-cream cones from the guy inside the Tastee-Freez truck and handing one to Gaia.

She took off half the ice cream from the top in one bite, shedding sprinkles all over the ground as she turned away from the truck. They strolled into the south entrance to Washington Square Park. It had turned into a seriously warm afternoon, and Jake had his jacket slung over the top of his duffel bag at his side. Gaia had slipped on a thin white T-shirt after her postfight shower, and she was still flushed from the heat of the water. Jake had to concentrate to keep from staring at her.

"Solid fight?" she said, her mouth full. "What happened to 'That was amazing'?"

"I was in the moment," Jake said, shrugging one shoulder as he approached an empty bench. Her fighting *had* been amazing, but there was no reason to let her know exactly how much he admired her. There was something to be said for playing one's cards close to the vest.

"So. . . what? You have criticisms?" Gaia asked as she sat down.

"A couple, maybe," he said nonchalantly. "But we don't have to talk about that now. We should be celebrating."

"We are," Gaia replied with a smile, lifting her cone slightly, as if in a toast.

Jake smiled back, then looked out across the park. Was it his imagination, or was Gaia a bit easier to be with this afternoon? She seemed friendlier somehow—less closed off. Was it even remotely possible that the connection he'd felt the day before hadn't been one-sided?

Usually Jake would be up front about his feelings

and just say something direct, like, "So, do you want to go out with me or what?" But somehow he didn't think it was time for that yet. He wasn't sure it would go over with Gaia the way it had gone over with girls in the past. There was something about her that made him... nervous. He wasn't used to that feeling, and he wasn't sure what to do with it yet.

But there was something else he wanted to talk to her about, anyway, and this good-mood thing might prove to be beneficial. He was just turning to her to ask her what was up with Tatiana when she cut him off.

"So... have you seen Tatiana lately?" she asked.

Jake's internal warning system went off and he looked away again. That question was just a little too out of the blue to mean nothing.

"Why?" he asked the park, before taking another bite of his ice cream.

"Just curious," she replied lightly.

Jake shook his head. "What the hell is going on with you two?" he asked. "What are you doing, playing some elaborate game of Charlie's Angels?"

Gaia turned her intense blue eyes on him. "So you have seen her," she stated.

"Yeah, I've seen her," Jake replied, growing angry. "And she told me that she wanted to see *you*. Said it was a matter of life or death."

Gaia's face flushed from hairline to jaw and she crunched into her cone.

"What is up with you guys? I thought you were friends! You were living together, for Christ's sake!" Jake blurted, as miffed that the light, happy vibe was ruined as he was over the fact that no one was telling him anything. He chucked the rest of his cone into a nearby garbage can and ran his hands through his short, dark hair.

"Come on, Gaia," he said, clenching his jaw. "Tell me what's going on here."

Gaia took a long, deep breath and let it out slowly. Jake could practically see the gears in her head turning. She was deciding what to say to him. Deciding whether to trust him or not. Why was she so afraid? He hadn't known her for long, but he'd never done anything to earn her mistrust.

She turned toward him again, and for one moment Jake thought she was going to talk to him. Really talk to him. Tell him what was going on and ask him for his help. It was pretty clear to him by now that one of the two girls in this situation really needed it.

Come on, Gaia, he thought. *Trust me.*

"Just. . . tell me where she is," Gaia said.

Jake deflated.

"I don't know where the hell she is!" Jake blurted. "This is ridiculous," he said, standing and grabbing up his bag. "I'm not going to get in the middle of whatever it is you two have going on. I've got my own crap to deal with."

Gaia narrowed her eyes. She stood up and squared

off with him, toe to toe, as if she were going to challenge him to a fight.

"One word of advice," she said tersely. "Don't trust Tatiana."

Jake threw his arms up and took a step back from her, laughing sarcastically. "How am I supposed to know which one of you I can trust when neither one of you is telling me shit?" he said.

His heart was thumping painfully, and he realized with a start that he was actually hurt. Hurt that she wouldn't trust him. The knowledge only pissed him off even more. He barely knew this girl. How had he managed to let himself get so involved?

Gaia picked up her bag, slung it over her head, and threw back her shoulders. "You're just going to have to figure that one out on your own," she said. "It's up to you."

Then she turned on her heel and walked away.

Damn. Damndamndamndamndamn.

I'm doing it again. I'm doing it again, even though I know I shouldn't be.

I think Jake's telling me the truth. I think he really doesn't know where Tatiana is and I think he did just tell me basically everything that mattered from their conversation, whenever it took place, wherever it took place. (She wants to see me—a matter of life and death.) There is nothing about this guy that isn't earnest and honest, even if he is the cockiest asshole ever to walk the earth. But at least he doesn't try to hide it. He is who he is. No apologies. How can you not admire a person like that? How can you not trust a person like that?

And there it is. I trust him. I'm doing it again. I'm trusting someone again, even though I know I shouldn't be.

Damn.

From: 322
To: L
Subject: Re: Total Recall

Agent 322 active. I await your directive.

saw herself

running down

the sidewalk

and launching

herself at Gaia,

saw the **hatred**

look of surprise

in those always-

in-control,

ever-superior

eyes

OLIVER STARED AT THE COMPUTER

Nerves of Steel

screen, trembling with excitement and nerves. A response. He'd finally received a response. So Loki's agents were still out there. Some of them, anyway. Part of him wasn't sure whether to be elated or disturbed. Here was an agent of his own alter ego's evil at his disposal, ready and waiting.

Oliver reached for the mouse but then drew back his hand. After two full days of sending messages and trying to hack into Loki's unhackable system, this small triumph was something he'd begun to take for granted as an impossibility. Now that someone had answered his call, he wasn't sure he was ready to deal with it. Was he really capable of being an evil mastermind?

The answer, he knew, was yes. That ability was somewhere inside him. And the last thing he wanted to do was light that particular powder keg.

But Loki isn't you. You are not him, Oliver told himself. *He can't come to the surface if you don't let him.*

Oliver took a sip from the water bottle Gaia had left with him that morning and tried to focus on the task at hand.

He was going to have to play this just right. This could be the most important mission of Oliver's life. And agent 322 was his only hope of completing that mission—of helping Gaia and finding Tom.

But what if he couldn't do it? What if he couldn't pass himself off as Loki?

Oliver leaned back and pressed his fingertips into his skull just above his eyes, cursing his own weakness. He was `petrified of failing`. Petrified of losing the only family he had left. He hated it, but there it was. If only he could have just an ounce of Gaia's fearlessness right now, it would certainly help him through this.

What had happened to the `nerves of steel` he'd developed during his years in the CIA? What had happened to his confidence—his ego? Had Loki appropriated all of that and left Oliver lacking? Was the real Oliver Moore now this broken shell of a man?

His hands shook as he drew himself up straight and cleared his throat.

"Pull yourself together," he whispered firmly, jumping his chair closer to the keyboard. Saying the words aloud bolstered his spirits somehow. When a person needed a pep talk and there was no one else around, he had to create his own pep. He clicked the reply button. "They're counting on you."

His fingertips hovered briefly over the keys, and then he began to type.

Status: Urgent, immediate attention imperative.
Mission: Locate Tom Moore, alias Enigma.
Current intel: Last seen Lenox Hill Hospital ICU,

```
may have been taken overseas. Was unconscious at
time of extraction.
```
Response: Critical. Meet for exchange at location
23F, tomorrow noon. Deadline is nonnegotiable.

Oliver read these few words over a dozen times before holding his breath and clicking the send button.

It's fine, he told himself as the message was shot irretrievably into the ether. No frills. No pleas. No signs of any weakness. Direct orders were definitely Loki's MO.

His breath caught in his throat when, one second after the order was sent, the computer bleeped, indicating that a message had been received. Operative 322 was sitting at his computer this very second, awaiting Loki's command. Praying that 322 hadn't figured him out the second he read his directive, Oliver opened the new mail.

```
Mission accepted.
```

A laugh bubbled up in Oliver's throat, and he let himself give in to his triumphant mirth. He folded his arms on the desk and rested his forehead on top of them, suddenly exhausted, relief flowing out of him with every body-racking guffaw. He'd done it. He'd finally done it. `Mission accomplished.` He could finally, *finally* relax. He felt his bones settle and crack as he let his posture sag and his muscles uncoil. It had been so long since he'd slept. . . .

A loud ringing suddenly pierced the air, and Oliver jumped back, startled. Other than muffled street noise, there had been no other sound in the brownstone since Gaia had left that morning. Heart in his throat, he grabbed the receiver to the desk phone and fumbled with it before bringing it to his face.

"What?" he barked.

A pause. Oliver saw his life flash before his eyes. They'd found him. They were coming for him. He was going to pay for all of Loki's sins.

"I'm sorry, is this Roger Simms?" a male voice asked on the other end of the line.

Roger Simms. That sounded so familiar. Why did he know that name. . . ?

"Mr. Simms?"

It hit Oliver like a brick to the head. Of course! Roger Simms. The name he'd used when calling locksmiths earlier that day. He was really going to have to get some food in him right away. There was no room for brainlessness in this game.

"Yes, yes," Oliver said, gripping the phone. "I'm sorry. And this is?"

"Reginald Toth, sir, of Chelsea Antiques," the man replied, taking on a clipped tone. "I believe I have some information for you on that key of yours."

Oliver grinned and pulled a pen and pad toward him. First 322 and now this. He was definitely on a roll, and each rotation brought him that much closer to earning Gaia's trust.

If he could just have that, there was nothing else he would ever need.

GAIA DRAGGED HER TIRED FEET UP

All Business

the cement steps to Oliver's brownstone and pushed open the front door. Since leaving Jake in Washington Square Park, she'd spent the bulk of the afternoon wandering Alphabet City with her eyes peeled, and she was definitely ready to crash.

But the second she stepped inside, she felt her pulse start to race. Oliver was waiting for her. He walked right over to her from the front window, where he'd clearly been watching for her return. The man hadn't been down from the fourth floor since they'd moved in here two days ago. Something was obviously up.

Just let it be good, whatever it is, Gaia thought, even as her brain told her that was highly unlikely. She tossed her bag on the dirt-and-cobweb-covered floor and crossed her arms over her chest.

"I have good news," Oliver said brightly. A phrase Gaia hadn't heard in ages.

"What is it?" she asked, letting the arms drop. "Did you find my dad?"

"Very nearly," Oliver said. He walked excitedly from the front hall into the spacious, empty living room. The blinds were drawn and the sun was going down, leaving the airy space gray and murky.

"What does 'very nearly' mean?" Gaia asked, following him, her mouth watering with anticipation.

"I've finally made contact with one of Loki's operatives," Oliver said, smiling. "He should have information for me at noon tomorrow."

Gaia swallowed hard and looked away, trying to hide the distrust that was written all over her face. She didn't like the idea of trusting Loki's men. Not after everything they'd done to her and to the people she loved. The very idea, in fact, made her skin crawl with a million little bugs of doubt. But she knew it was the only way. She was just going to have to accept it.

"That's. . . great," she said finally.

"That's just the beginning," Oliver said, taking a few steps closer to her. He pulled a couple of squares of paper from his back pocket and unfolded them. "Information about your key."

The papers fluttered slightly as he held them out to her, and Gaia could relate—her heart was pretty much doing the same thing. She grabbed the sheets and looked them over quickly. There were names, dates, building code numbers, recall numbers, and on the last page Oliver had written in huge block letters:

Between Avenues A & D, East 2nd–East 5th.

Gaia's mind spun. "Does this mean what I think it means?" she asked, looking up at him.

Oliver smiled a knowing, almost cocky smile. He was proud of his detective work.

"It turns out that type of lock was used only in early–twentieth-century developments in the Meat Packing District and in Alphabet City. They were taken off the market when a fault was found in the pin system," Oliver explained. "If we're right about an Alphabet City safe house, then it's somewhere within those blocks."

Gaia quickly did the math, a grid of lower Manhattan appearing in her mind's eye. Sixteen city blocks. That was all the area she needed to search. Tatiana was somewhere within sixteen measly city blocks.

Oliver held out the key to her, and Gaia grabbed it from his hand, already plotting out the subway stops she'd need to sit through before she got where she needed to be.

"Thank you," Gaia said, folding up the papers and stuffing them into her pocket. Oliver didn't move, and just before she turned to go, Gaia felt a sudden charge in the air. Like something was expected. Like he wanted something.

She glanced at him, and his softened eyes told the story. He was waiting for more than thanks. He wanted a reaction. He wanted elation. He wanted awe and congratulations. In fact, he was looking at her like he wanted a hug.

Gaia's stomach twisted with a combination of guilt, disgust, and pity. She knew this was Oliver standing before her, but the very idea of hugging him—of touching the body that played home to Loki—was physically repulsive. Her heart went out to Oliver but shrank from his evil alter ego.

She wasn't yet ready for contact.

"Thanks," Gaia said again, forcing a smile. "Really."

Oliver lifted his chin and looked away for a split second, and she knew he was consciously arranging his features. When he gazed at her again, he was collected—all business.

"Just watch your back," he said. "Natasha will have taken other measures to secure the safe house."

"Don't worry," Gaia replied firmly.

She clasped the key in her palm and headed for the door, her adrenaline running high. Whatever Natasha had in store for her, she could handle. The only thing that mattered now was finding Tatiana and finding out what she knew. The chase was on.

One Step Ahead

TATIANA WHIPPED A YANKEES BASEBALL cap out of her backpack and pulled it down low on her forehead, cursing Jake under her breath. She'd just spent two hours sitting in the café that time forgot, waiting for his curiosity to get the better of him and for him to come looking for her. The place had Frank Sinatra's greatest hits on an endless loop and sold nothing with caffeine other than bad coffee and generic cola. She'd picked Café Mille Lucci as her rendezvous point because all kinds of people were in and out of the place all day—young, old, poor, not so poor, every race imaginable. It was the perfect place to become just another one of the many. The only problem was, the atmosphere and the food sucked.

She stalked around a corner and almost leveled a scary-looking Hispanic man with track marks all up and down his arms. He shouted right in her face, but she quickly sidestepped him and kept walking, head down. Whenever she went to the café, she had to go wigless so that if Jake showed up, he wouldn't get more suspicious than he already was. But every time she left the safe house as herself, she was taking a risk. The last thing she needed was another Megan-type debacle. She was supposed to be invisible here.

"I shouldn't even have to *be* here anymore," Tatiana muttered, watching her feet as she walked.

She should have known that she couldn't count on Jake. At least Brendan was predictable and thus reliable. He was either in the bar or at the McDonald's down the street for about twenty hours out of every day. Maybe it was time she just got him and his stupid friends to kidnap Gaia from school. At this point it was probably the best plan she had going. Which wasn't saying much.

Tatiana took a deep, calming breath as she ducked around the last corner and her safe house came into view. All she had to do was get inside, sit down, chill out, and come up with a plan B. Jake might have failed her, but that didn't mean she was down and out. She wouldn't give up that easily.

A few doors down a group of men in puffy black jackets and do-rags stood on a stoop as always, chatting with each other and blowing smoke into the air. Tatiana abhorred this part of the day. Every time she walked past these guys, no matter what getup she was sporting, they hooted and howled and made smooching noises and lewd remarks until she was out of sight. She was just steeling herself for the onslaught when she saw something that made her stop dead in her tracks.

Gaia.

Tatiana leaned forward to get a better look at the

guy with the gold tooth who was gesturing with his cigarette. Tatiana's fight-or-flight reflex was telling her to get the hell out of there as fast as possible, but then her self-preservation kicked in and she realized that any sudden movement would draw big-time notice. Thanking God for her own split-second sanity, she slipped behind the corner newsstand and flattened herself against its rickety wall, waiting for her pulse to slow.

But it wouldn't. Gaia was here. Gaia was in her neighborhood. The little supersleuth had tracked her down. But how? *How?* It just wasn't possible. Tatiana had all the advantages in this situation, yet Gaia, as always, was somehow one step ahead.

Pulse pounding in her ears, Tatiana risked a peek around the side of the newsstand, and her jaw clenched. There she was, listening intently, her perfect brow wrinkled in concentration like that of a good little reporter. Oh, how Tatiana hated her. Hated her for her condescension, for her abilities, for her fearlessness, for the fact that she always had the edge. Her fingers curled into fists, and she saw herself stepping out of her hiding place, saw herself running down the sidewalk and launching herself at Gaia, saw the look of surprise in those always-in-control, ever-superior eyes.

What she wouldn't give to be able to kick the living crap out of the girl right here and now.

Tatiana took a long breath and fought it. She fought the urge that was overwhelming every cell in her body. Because if she did what she wanted to do, it was her own ass that would get kicked. It wasn't fair, but it was true. It was just one more edge that belonged to Gaia.

Ever so slowly Tatiana pulled herself behind the newsstand again, her anger rushing out of her, leaving nothing but a sucking hole of loneliness in its place. Loneliness and fear—something Gaia would never have to face.

Tatiana thought of her mother. She was out there somewhere right now, probably in pain, probably scared and being as brave as possible, probably worried for Tatiana's life. And here Tatiana was, doing everything she could, but Gaia was still going to win. She was already well on her way.

It's not fair, Tatiana thought, feeling her resolve slipping away—feeling her strength escape her. *It's just not fair. . . .*

She knew that she needed to stay strong. She knew that the situation demanded it. But no one was here. Not a soul would witness it if she cracked. And for the moment she couldn't do it anymore. Not alone. It was too much.

And so while Gaia questioned every person on the street, coming closer and closer to her mark, Tatiana slid down the wall of the newsstand, pulled her knees up under her chin, and wept.

CURIOSITY KILLED THE MORON, JAKE

Two and Two

told himself as he approached the door to Café Mille Lucci, his brain trying to convince him one last time that this was a bad idea. But he couldn't help it. All he'd done all afternoon was go over and over his last conversations with Gaia and Tatiana, trying to put two and two together. The only problem was, he had yet to come up with four.

Someone was going to explain what was going on, and they were going to do it now. It was their choice to suck him into their little drama, so one of them was going to have to talk. And since he had a feeling it wasn't going to be Gaia, he'd decided to start with Tatiana.

He yanked open the door and readied himself for an inquisition, but the moment he saw Tatiana, he faltered. She was slouched in a booth, her back up against the wall and one leg up on the vinyl bench. Streaks of dried tears cut rivers down her face, and there were circles of smudged makeup beneath her eyes. Her gaze was unfocused and staring, and her skin looked sallow under the fluorescent lights.

Jake's mind flashed on an image of his mother before she died, when she was weak and tired and helpless and he couldn't do anything for her. When she would just lie there in that hospital bed, looking at him with those sorrowful eyes, and he was just a little

167

kid who could do nothing. Suddenly every muscle in his body tensed up. He had to do something.

"Tatiana?" he said, walking over to the edge of her bench.

Her eyes slowly traveled up to meet his face, but she showed no sign of recognition. Okay, this was worse than he thought.

"Hey! Tatiana!" he said a bit louder, crouching by her sneaker that hung over the edge of the bench. "Are you okay?"

She inhaled, the breath choppy through an obviously stuffy nose. She looked off past his ear at some distant, probably nonexistent point.

"Hey! Can I get some cold water over here?" Jake called out over his shoulder.

An elderly waitress heaved a sigh and left her magazine at the counter to go wrangle up some ice water. Jake watched her progress with an ever-growing swell of impatience in his chest. When she finally handed him the glass, ice cubes tinkling, he gave her a sarcastic smile.

"Thanks a lot," he said tonelessly.

He dipped his fingers into the water, reached over, and flicked it into Tatiana's face. She blinked and shook her head and seemed to wake up.

"Jake!" she said, finally focusing. Then she sat up and started to cry.

"Hey! What the hell is going on?" Jake asked, sitting down next to her. Tatiana collapsed into him like a marionette whose strings had just been severed, crying quietly. Before he knew it, he found himself wrapping his arms around her, stroking her hair, and whispering a repetitive mantra of "It's going to be all right. . . . It's going to be all right. . . . It's going to be all right."

"You have to help me, Jake," she choked out through her tears. "Please. You're the only one who can."

Against his will, Jake was moved by Tatiana's total transformation from together, *über*-social queen bee to `helpless victim`. Whatever was going on between Gaia and Tatiana, this girl needed help.

"Okay," he said. "Okay. I'll do whatever I can."

Guys are so easy. They fall for sex, they fall for tears, they fall for the silent treatment, they fall for jealousy, they fall for disinterest. There are any number of things you can do to manipulate a guy. The key is knowing the guy well enough. Is he a knight in shining armor, a child, a lecher, a man who needs a challenge? Not all of the above tactics will work on all men—you have to mix and match.

Brendan, for example, is clearly the sex type. He isn't going to be swooping in to save any damsels in distress—he'd probably think that blubbering was funny. And he's not the type to waste his time with someone who isn't giving him the proper signals. So sex it was. And it worked.

Jake, on the other hand, is a total hero. He may put on a tough act, but he so wants to be the savior guy. It's written all over his face. So tears, of course, worked.

That's the difference between

me and Gaia—I understand guys.
Think she would ever break down
in front of Jake? Please. She'd
sooner die than admit she needed
to be saved.

And so I do still have an
edge. A small one, but an important one.

He was
trying to
make Gaia
jealous....**stare**
Unfortunately,
it was
working.

BRENDAN WAS HUNCHED ON THE LAST

Undergarment Action

bar stool, one beefy arm resting along the edge of the bar, the other curled around a mug of beer like it was a bunny rabbit or a kitten—something to be cuddled and protected. From the lolling of his head and the constant movement of his lips, Tatiana could tell that he was sloshed, three sheets to the wind, completely blasted.

She clenched her fists and told herself to remain calm. These were the pitfalls of aligning oneself with shady characters like Brendan. All she could do was hope that he was cognizant enough to hear what she had to say and remember it. She unbuttoned the third button on her white blouse, exposing a hint of the lace bra underneath. Maybe a little `undergarment action` would rouse him enough to pay attention.

Tatiana walked over to Brendan and slipped onto the stool next to his, making sure her leg brushed his. He swung his big head to the left and grinned stupidly when he saw her.

"It's the siren," he said, lifting his beer mug and downing half the contents. He slammed it back down onto the bar, and Tatiana slid it away from him, placing it at arm's reach on her other side. He swiveled his bar stool so he could better see her. Tatiana watched, careful to control all visceral reaction, as his eyes slid down her neck to her cleavage. She leaned forward slightly to give him a better look.

"The plan is on," she said. She placed her hands on either side of his grizzly chin and lifted his face so that he'd have to look at her. It took a couple of extra seconds for his eyes to catch up with his chin. Tatiana smiled. "I need you to bring as much firepower as possible to the Hiro Dojo on West Eleventh Street tonight, nine o'clock."

Brendan's red-rimmed eyes swam. "That's where we're doing this?" he said, spitting a bit. "A freakin' dojo? What is this, *Karate Kid?*" He leaned back on his stool precariously and waved his hands around in the air. "Wax on! Wax off!" Then he collapsed on the bar, laughing at his own stupid joke.

Tatiana pressed her teeth together, waiting for him to finish convulsing.

"It's a believable location for my bait to lure our mark to," she said when he finally lifted his eyes. She raised one shoulder, thereby exposing a bit more breast, then reached over and trailed a fingertip along the back of his hand. "He's setting it all up. It'll be deserted, and he has a key." She looked flirtatiously into his eyes. "I'm good at what I do, Brendan."

He leered predictably. "I'll bet you are."

"So, you'll be where, when?" she asked him.

"Hiro Dojo, West Eleventh, nine o'clock tonight," he replied, looming so close, she could pick out the various alcoholic substances on his breath.

"Very good," she replied, smiling through her disgust.

"And when the job's done, I get my promised payment, right?" he asked, his hand falling clumsily on her upper thigh.

"Definitely," Tatiana replied. Holding her breath, she leaned in and kissed Brendan. His tongue fought its way into her mouth as he kissed her back violently. Tatiana silently counted to ten, then pulled away with some effort. Brendan nearly fell off his bar stool.

"I never break a promise," Tatiana said, the sour taste of him all over her. She passed him his beer in an effort to distract him, and he tilted his head over it, staring into its coppery depths. Tatiana headed for the door, fishing a roll of breath mints out of her bag.

"OKAY, OLD MAN," OLIVER SAID UNDER

322 his breath, stopping his hands from trembling by stuffing them into the pockets of his gray trench coat. "Okay. You're fine. You can pull this off."

He stood in the darkest corner of the alleyway between Kavlav's Gyros and Song's House of Nails, trying to avoid breathing in the acrid mix of frying lamb and nail polish remover. The height of the buildings blocked out the sun, and the extra shadow cast by the Dumpster next to him provided a perfect haven. He had arrived fifteen minutes early for his meet in order to be there when 322 arrived. This was what Loki had always done to keep his operatives on their toes, so this was what Oliver had to do.

He heard a footstep, a crunch of gravel, and held his breath, telling himself not to peek. If it was his operative, he would know the protocol. There was no need to reveal himself if it was anyone else.

Noisy rustling in the garbage cans down the alley ensued, and Oliver knew he had time. Agent 322 wouldn't enter if there was a homeless person rooting through the trash. He would have to wait it out.

Naturally, his thoughts turned to Gaia. He knew she didn't fully trust him yet—had seen the way she looked at him with a protective veil over her eyes. She was probably wondering when Loki would resurface, whether she'd be able to tell the difference when he did, whether he already had. Oliver knew these suspicions were well founded—ingrained, even. He knew they were justified.

All he had to do now was erase them forever. He needed Gaia to trust him. She was all he had.

The banging and rustling stopped, and the footsteps gradually moved away. Oliver knew that the next few moments would decide his fate. If he could convince 322 that he was Loki, he would gain the information that would help Gaia. And once he had the information, she would know he was good. She would know that he lived to help her—that he was worthy of being called "uncle."

If 322 didn't believe him, however, all was lost.

More footsteps, quieter this time but authoritative. No timorous sneaking around. This was it. Oliver could feel it. A cold tingling sensation ran down his back. And there it was.

Scrape. . . scrape. . . scrape. The sound of a shoe sole being dragged carefully back and forth. The signal.

Oliver steeled himself and stepped out into the light.

"Boss," 322 said. He stood a few yards away, dressed in head-to-toe black, a baseball cap pulled down over his brow, exposing nary a hair on his head. His eyes were hidden behind dark sunglasses.

"The file," Oliver said flatly.

322 produced a large envelope from behind his back. He took the few steps necessary to close the distance between him and Oliver and handed over the envelope. He then took two respectful steps back and stood at ease.

Loki slipped open the envelope and glanced

177

inside. A few sheets of paper, an eight-by-ten photograph. A computer disk. He could hardly restrain himself from shaking the items out into his hand, but he found the strength. He cleared his throat and resealed the envelope.

"Good work," he said.

His words seemed to open a floodgate within the operative. "Where've you been, boss? The organization is a wreck. There have been so many defections. . . . How did you escape?"

Oliver's mind spun with possible explanations, lies, details. He could weave a plausible story in no time— one aspect of his CIA training that hadn't deserted him. He was about to unleash a web of deceit when he caught himself. No. Wrong.

"That's none of your concern," he snapped, causing 322 to go pale. "There may have been defections, but you have proved your loyalty here today." He tucked the envelope under his arm. "Your work will not go unnoticed. Now go."

The operative let a bit of a smile escape his lips, then he nodded once and slipped out of the alley. Oliver breathed a long sigh of relief. He'd pulled it off.

Clutching the envelope to his breast, Oliver strode from the alley and turned his steps toward the subway. He would wait until he was home to open the envelope again. There he would be able to peruse the contents safely and, hopefully, rejoice over his success.

Giving the Eye

GAIA STARED AT MRS. BACKER AS SHE walked back and forth in front of the classroom, lecturing about the Battle of the Bulge. Whatever the teacher was saying, she was very excited about it—gesturing, pausing for drama, throwing in her own sound effects here and there. "Boom! Argh! Move the line! Move the line!" Gaia was sure she would be riveted if she could remotely focus on what the woman was saying.

But she couldn't. All she could focus on was the fact that Jake had been staring at her for precisely thirty-nine minutes now without a break. He sat less than two feet away from her, and his eyes were riveted on her face, his chin resting on his arms, which were stacked on top of his desk. Greg Marshall's sizable frame blocked Jake from Backer's sight, making it all the easier for him to do this. To s t a r e . To drive her totally stir-crazy.

What the hell did he *know?* And why was he giving her the eye? Had she been wrong to trust him?

Gaia turned her head away from Jake toward the windows on the other side of the room and froze. Ed. He was staring at her, too. The second she caught his eye, he glanced at Jake, reddened, then turned in his seat to face the front.

Oh, this *is really fun,* Gaia thought, her heart convulsing.

But she couldn't deal with Ed's feelings right now. She'd talked to him, and he knew how she felt. Besides, Jake's unbreakable stare was a little too distracting to let her focus on anything else at that moment.

Gaia shifted in her seat, sitting up slightly and tapping her pen against the edge of her history book. Out of the corner of her eye she saw Jake's gaze follow her face. She colored slightly. What was this guy's *deal?*

It occurred to her that if she were to go completely against her instincts and *not* trust Jake, then he and Tatiana could be scheming against her. It was totally plausible that Jake knew *exactly* where Tatiana was. That he knew what her next move would be. That he would help her make it.

All of which would completely suck, considering the fact that Gaia was just beginning to like the guy.

Gaia sighed and glanced at the clock. Just over a minute left. Backer seemed to be coming to the climax of the battle, swinging her arms up over her head and down, her eyes bulging as she ranted.

There was one other angle to consider here. Maybe Jake was just an innocent do-gooder. Maybe he was simply a good friend. Tatiana could be feeding him some line about an estrangement between herself and Gaia. She could be playing him like a harmonica. And maybe, just maybe, Jake just wanted to help. Maybe he thought he *was* helping—both her *and* Tatiana.

Maybe Jake was really just a good guy. Somehow that was the easiest scenario to believe.

The bell rang and Gaia stood up, sliding her books into her hand. She hadn't taken one step when Jake's fingers closed around her bicep. Ah. So this was going to go beyond ogling. Gaia saw Ed pause by the door, jealousy and concern flitting over his face before he ducked his head and slipped from the room. Gaia ignored the sour feeling in her chest over the hurt she was causing Ed and turned to face Jake. She could deal with her warring emotions later. For now she had to deal with all her other problems.

"Are you going to let me go?" Gaia asked.

Jake started to speak, then stopped himself. He released her arm and adjusted his books from one hand to the other and rested them against his hip, watching the exchange as if it took great care.

"What's up?" Gaia asked, impatient.

Jake glanced at Mrs. Backer, who was straightening her desk at the front of the room. Then he tilted his head toward the door and started to move. Gaia followed him out into the crowded hallway, where he paused near the wall. He looked around, and Gaia did the same, then wished she hadn't. Ed was standing right across from them against the other wall, talking to the same girl he'd attended the match with the day before. She had obviously been waiting for him outside of class. Ed glanced in Gaia and Jake's direction, saw Gaia watching, then reached out and pushed the girl's hair behind her ear.

It was a shameless act. He was trying to make Gaia jealous because he was jealous of Jake. Unfortunately, it was working.

Focus, Gaia told herself. *You want Ed to move on. You practically told him to do this. You'll get over it.*

"Well?" she said to Jake impatiently.

Ed and the girl moved across the hall until they were standing right behind Jake. The girl started to twirl the lock on the locker about five feet away.

Perfect, Gaia thought sarcastically. *Now Ed's going to hear. . . whatever Jake's going to say.*

Jake lifted his chin and looked her right in the eye. "I was wondering if you'd meet me somewhere tonight," he said.

He was tense. He blinked about a hundred times. He reached up and scratched over his ear. Telltale signs that there was more going on here than he was saying.

Gaia's heart sank, but she didn't have time to dwell on it. This was it. Tatiana had gotten to him. Well, fine. At least she knew who her friends were, and at least it was almost over.

"Sure," Gaia said with an easy smile. "Where do you want to go?"

From: Y
To: X22
Subject: Subject L

Reactivation confirmed. Major breach. Have assigned my personal team to subject L's movements. This is a debacle. This is unacceptable. Any informant on the breakdown of communication in this matter will be rewarded.

The responsible parties will answer for this with their lives.

If there
was ever
a time
to play
the
superhero,   **karate**
this   **chop**
was it.

ED GLANCED AT HIS WATCH AS HE
waited outside the rest rooms at the Union Square Theater. It was eight fifty-five. In five minutes Gaia was going to be meeting Jake a couple of blocks away to do. . . whatever it was they were going to do. And Kai was in the bathroom, taking a very long time.

"Come on, Kai," Ed said under his breath. "What are you doing in there?"

The door opened and a pretty brunette walked out. She took the hand of one of the other guys waiting along the wall, and they walked toward the door together, laughing.

I'm evil, Ed thought, watching the happy couple. *Kai asked me to go to a movie and I set the whole thing up at this specific theater at this specific time just so I could spy on Gaia and Jake. What kind of date am I?*

Of course, Kai did live somewhere in this neighborhood, so it wasn't like the choice of theater was out of her way. Plus he wasn't totally certain that he and Kai were *on* a date. Maybe they were just two people hanging at the movies together. And if that was the case, he didn't have to worry about the fact that he was obsessively stalking his ex.

Uh-huh. Sure.

"Hey!" Kai said, emerging from the bathroom. "Ready to go?"

"Uh. . . yeah," Ed said glancing at his watch again.

Maybe he should just bag it. Maybe he should walk out the front door of this theater and make a right instead of a left. Walk away from the address he'd overheard Jake give Gaia that afternoon.

But he knew he wouldn't. He had to see what the two of them were doing. He had to know if she'd broken his heart just to date someone else.

"So, what did you think of the movie?" Kai asked as they pushed through the glass doors at the Union Square Theater and were accosted by the scent of roasting nuts and toasting pretzels from a nearby vendor.

"It was supremely bad," Ed said, surprised at his own ability to make normal small talk when his heart was racing. "I mean, that was on par with *Saving Silverman* and *Scooby-Doo*."

"You didn't like *Scooby-Doo*?" Kai blurted, eyebrows raised.

"You did?" Ed asked over his shoulder as he crossed the street. "I just lost all respect for you."

"Please! You have to leave some room for movies you can laugh *at* as well as *with*," Kai replied, giggling. "There's value in that."

Ed tilted his head, trying not to be too obvious about looking around for a glimpse of Gaia or Jake. He was close enough to their meeting spot that he might catch one of them approaching.

"Huh. Never looked at it that way," he said. "In that

case, *Episode Two* is a classic and Hayden Christiansen is my favorite comedic actor."

Kai laughed and skipped to catch up with him. She linked her arm through his, and Ed glanced down at her pink-gloved hand, surprised. Huh. So apparently this *was* a date. And he was happy to note that, even in his slightly neurotic state of mind, Kai's gesture sent a little warm tingle through his arm.

Of course, the tingle was quickly followed by a massive wave of guilt. Kai was cool. She was talkative, happy, fun. She had this optimistic take on pretty much everything from the flatness of her soda ("Bubbles sometimes make me sneeze, which is, like, so rude in a movie theater") to the fact that she'd stepped in gum ("At least the poor usher guy doesn't have to scrape it up now").

This was new and different. A girl who saw the good. A girl who touched him without a huge internal debate. A girl he could actually *date* instead of fruitlessly pursue to the point of exhaustion and ultimate multiple heart-breakings.

A girl who was too cool to be used in the way that Ed was currently using her. Ed paused in the middle of the sidewalk. That was it. He couldn't do this to her. He wasn't going to go looking for Gaia in the middle of his first date with Kai.

"Why are you stopping?" Kai asked.

Ed looked north toward the park. "I was thinking. . . .

You want to go get something to eat at Coffee Shop or something?" Coffee Shop was on Fifteenth Street, in the opposite direction from the place Gaia and Jake were meeting. In the *healthy* direction.

"Actually, I kind of have to get home," Kai said, wincing. "My mom's a nutcase when it comes to school night curfews."

Ed smiled and pulled her a little closer to him. "Well, then, I'll walk you home," he said. "Where's your place again?"

"I'm on Sixth Avenue and Tenth," Kai replied. "We can cut down here."

She started off toward Eleventh Street, but Ed didn't move. "Uh. . . why don't we walk down Twelfth?" he asked.

"You feeling okay?" Kai asked. "Why go up to come back?"

Good question, Ed thought. *Can't answer, "Because if we go down Eleventh, we may see my ex with her new boyfriend, which I've just decided would be bad."*

"Come on," Kai said, tugging at his arm. "I want to stop at the market down here, anyway, and stock up on gum."

Just go. She's going to think you're a psycho, Ed told himself.

He fell into step with Kai and took the turn down Eleventh Street, his heart pounding, hoping his stall tactics had eaten up a few minutes. Maybe he had already missed the happy couple. Maybe he wouldn't even have to see—

Gaia.

Ed stopped short, causing Kai to almost lose her footing, when he saw Gaia walking along the other side of the street. Her shoulders were slumped forward and her head was down, but her eyes were on high alert. She was staring at the door to a building a few doors up from her—a dojo—and she was tense.

She was definitely not in a nervous I'm-meeting-a-guy frame of mind. She was in a defensive I'm-watching-my-back frame of mind.

"What's up?" Kai asked, her brow wrinkling. "Oh, no. Did those Sour Patch Kids just hit your stomach?"

"No. I'm all right," Ed replied, ripping his eyes from Gaia long enough to give Kai a reassuring smile.

Gaia looked around her before ducking into the alley next to the dojo. Something was up. Ed could feel his Gaia-danger radar going off. This wasn't a date—this was something else. Something not good. And Ed didn't even register relief over the fact that she wasn't in for a night of romance. His first instinct was to follow her—find out what was going on and whether he could help.

But where had that gotten him in the past? Almost killed a few times, that's where. And all his interference ever did for Gaia was annoy her. She could handle herself. And she *was* meeting Jake here. He could protect her. Not that Ed could ever imagine Gaia needing protection.

"You *sure* you're all right?" Kai asked skeptically. She popped her gum.

"I'm fine," Ed replied. He turned his back on the dojo and started walking again. Kai leaned over and rested her head on his shoulder as they strolled, and Ed took a deep breath.

I'm fine, Ed repeated silently—firmly. *I'm just moving on.*

GAIA CLIMBED THE CEMENT STAIRS

to the back door of the dojo, her thick-soled boots crunching through the thin layer of silt on the steps. As Jake had promised, **Yin-Yang** the place was deserted—no classes battling it out inside, not a soul in sight. A fading yin-yang symbol was painted on the wooden door at the top of the stairs. Gaia pressed her ear against it and heard nothing. When she turned the knob, the door swung open easily.

The place was pitch black. Gaia stepped into the large, airy room, moving only inches from the door. It was freezing inside, as if someone had left the air conditioning on full blast, but the hair on Gaia's neck wasn't standing on end because of the chill. Someone was here—she could feel it.

"Jake?" she called out.

Before her question stopped echoing, someone grabbed her from behind. Her arms were pinned back, and as much as Gaia struggled, she couldn't free herself.

So here it is, she thought. *Ambush time.* Apparently Tatiana had made herself some friends while she was on the lam. Some friends other than Jake.

"Ooh. . . feisty," a growling voice said in her ear, accompanied by the thick stench of scotch.

Gaia wrinkled her nose in disgust and stopped trying to pull away. The guy seemed to like the struggling. And besides, she had a feeling he wasn't going to kill her. Not just yet. Tatiana was here somewhere, and she was going to want to show herself to Gaia before she died. She was going to want to gloat over her victory.

Gaia's assailant shoved her into a chair and proceeded to hold her down while some other person used thick ropes to bind her. Her hands were tied around the back of the chair, straining her arm muscles, and her ankles were each tied to a chair leg. As they worked, Gaia strained her ears to hear whether there were more people in the darkness, and there were. At least two—maybe more.

The two men stepped away from Gaia, satisfied that she was going nowhere, and the lights flickered on. Gaia blinked against the sudden brightness. When she was able to focus again, she saw that five men, mostly in jeans and distressed suede and leather, surrounded her, each with his own special sneer and each with his own special gun aimed at her face. A couple of them looked strong, and most of them had the glassy eyes of total drunks. Gaia looked past them to the thick black velvet curtains that lined the two side walls, and then the door to the dojo's office opened and out walked Tatiana, her boots clicking on the polished wooden floor. She was wearing a short, dark wig, but it was definitely her.

Gaia felt her blood start to race in her veins at the sight of her. Before this night was over, she was going to wipe that smirk off little Tatiana's face.

Ever so dramatically, Tatiana stepped across the room until she was face-to-face with Gaia but a few yards away. She flicked her blue eyes to each of her thugs, smiling a bit more each time, as if to draw Gaia's attention to them—as if to say, "I've got you now."

Gaia took a deep breath, sighed, and adopted her most bored expression.

Tatiana's eyes narrowed. "You're going to tell me where my mother is," she said, her voice filling the room.

Gaia's lips twitched. "No. You're going to tell me where my father is."

"I don't think you're in any position to make demands," Tatiana snapped.

Gaia's smile widened. "I wouldn't say that."

"NOW!" JAKE SHOUTED.

Unarmed

He ripped away the black curtain that shrouded his face and stepped out into the dojo in perfect unison with nine of his closest, most powerful friends. He took in the scene quickly. Gaia was tied to a chair in the center of the room, Tatiana was looking at him, shocked, and five huge guys with guns were just turning around to take aim at the fighters who lined the walls. Jake and his friends had the gun toters surrounded, but they were also unarmed.

"Dude, no one said anything about guns," Jake's friend Thomas said through his teeth.

You read my mind, Jake thought, trying not to let his fear show. Who *were* these girls?

Suddenly Tatiana reached behind her back and pulled a gun out of her waistband, aiming for Jake.

"Down!" Jake called out.

He dropped to the floor and rolled into the legs of the nearest guy, taking him down just as he fired his first shot—into the ceiling. After that, everything was a blur and Jake was moving on pure instinct. The guy's gun went skittering across the floor and slid under the curtains. He struggled to get up, but Jake and his sparring partner from the dojo, Derek, made sure he stayed down. It was almost too easy. The guy was clearly trashed, and he didn't have much fight in him. A one-two punch from Derek, followed by an elbow jab to the back from Jake, and the dude had passed out on the floor, sleeping like a baby.

"No!" Tatiana yelled out over the sounds of fired shots and landed punches, the groans and grunts and shouts of the battle. "No! No! No!"

Jake glanced in her direction and saw that Christov had easily disarmed her before moving on to his next opponent. Tatiana was stomping her feet like a spoiled child.

Jake and Derek rose up into their fighting stances and surveyed the room. The big guy who'd arrived first with Tatiana was giving a couple of Jake's friends a hard time on the far side of the room.

"You help Tim," Jake said, feeling not unlike an army general giving orders. It gave him a bit of a high. `If there was ever a time to play the superhero, this was it.` This was his moment. "I'm gonna get Gaia," he added.

Derek nodded and ran across the room. Jake rushed over to Gaia and fell on his knees at her side. He yanked his switchblade from the back pocket of his jeans and went to work on the ropes that bound her wrists.

Jake Montone to the rescue! a little voice in his brain shouted. *Super-Jake! Jake the Great. . .*

"You carry a knife?" Gaia said, her voice strained.

"Only when I need to," Jake replied. "You all right?" he asked as he sawed at the ropes.

"Been better," Gaia replied.

Something about the way she said it made Jake's heart stop short in his chest. He pulled back a little and surveyed her body, making sure she wasn't hurt. There was a large stain of blood on the leg of her jeans, and it was spreading.

"Oh my God. You're shot," he said, grabbing for her leg.

"Leave it," Gaia demanded. "It's just a scratch."

One of the thugs went flying over their heads and landed on his back with a loud moan. Jake still couldn't believe this was happening. When Gaia had told him that Tatiana was setting them both up, he'd had no idea she was going to bring her own little army.

"Jake, please," she said. "Tatiana. . ."

He glanced around and saw Tatiana searching the guy who'd just been tossed—shoving her hands frantically into his pockets and feeling along his legs. She was looking for a gun.

"Got it," Jake said, his adrenaline pumping.

He sliced through the last threads of the fraying ropes and Gaia swung her arms free. Her eyes were trained on Tatiana, and Jake could tell she was salivating to get to the girl, but her legs were still bound. Jake stood up, grabbed the back of the chair, and ripped it off the seat, tossing the shredded wood across the room.

"Can you stand?" he asked Gaia.

Tatiana was now crawling around the room, feeling under the curtains. She was only yards away from the first thug's gun.

Gaia grunted her approval and struggled up. The moment her butt was up, Jake sliced the wooden seat in two with one expertly placed karate chop. The seat fell free of the chair legs and he was able to pull the two rods of wood out of the ropes around Gaia's ankles.

As soon as Gaia was free, she spun around, her eyes searching. She spotted something and dove past Jake toward the back wall. At the same moment Tatiana finally found her gun and whirled around as she stood, her wig falling from her head, her eyes wild.

"Gaia!" Jake shouted.

But he didn't need to alert her. She'd found her own weapon and aimed it right back at Tatiana. The two girls cocked their guns at the same time and stood there, chests heaving, at opposite sides of the room, an Old West-style standoff.

Okay, Jake thought. *This is not your ordinary catfight.*

He had no idea what was going to happen next, but he had the distinct feeling that it was not going to be good. His friends from the dojo, having made short work of Tatiana's little band of thugs, walked up behind him. They all stood there and watched the two girls in silent awe.

"You don't see that every day," Derek whispered just off Jake's shoulder.

"No, you don't," Jake replied.

"We're not going to solve this if we're both dead," Gaia said, her shooting arm as steady as a tree branch.

"No, we're not," Tatiana agreed.

"I don't want to shoot you," Gaia said.

There was a beat. "Nor I you," Tatiana replied.

She blinked. She was lying. In that moment Jake knew for absolute certain that Tatiana wanted Gaia dead. Gaia had warned him that this was the case earlier this afternoon when he told her about this meeting and had been honest about who was calling it. That was why he'd agreed to bring along his friends. That was why he was here. But he'd never fully believed it until that moment. Tatiana wanted to kill Gaia. The girl really was a psycho.

"So why don't we just both put down our guns and talk this out?" Gaia suggested. "I'll tell you what I know about your mom, you tell me what you know about my dad."

Tatiana took a deep breath. "Agreed," she said.

Ever so slowly both girls lowered their arms and crouched to the floor to put down their guns. Gaia winced in pain and grabbed at her leg, and Jake's heart flew into his throat. He glanced at Tatiana, and she saw her opportunity. She reached behind her, and Jake caught a glimpse of silver—the butt of another gun—tucked into the waistband of her pants.

"No!" Jake shouted, and took off across the room.

One step and Tatiana had the gun in her hands.

The second step and she was training it on Gaia.

The third step and he swore he heard the catch of the trigger.

He threw himself into the air, his eyes locked on Gaia's shocked face. The sound of the gunshot exploded in his ears, and then `everything went black.`

Tonight, I swear on my life, I remembered what it was like to learn to walk. The first time, that is. Not the last time, after I got out of my wheelchair. I swear, I vividly remembered being one year old and concentrating my little diapered ass off as I tried to walk to my father's outstretched arms. Only this time I was concentrating to walk away from someone. And it took everything I had.

It's unbelievable, that thin line between love and hate. That tiny little thin line is like a balance beam that's. . . well, impossible to walk.

But somehow I did it. I put one foot in front of the other, and somehow I made it to the end of the block and got Kai to her building.

And then I took that last monster step. I kissed Kai good night.

And it wasn't half bad.

She thought of
Jake's open,
honest face. . .
the way he'd
looked at **heart**
her as he
threw **monitor**
himself in the
path of the bullet
that was meant for
her heart.

GAIA PULLED THE METAL-AND-PLASTIC

Grub

chair over to the side of Jake's hospital bed and sat facing his side, watching the little line on his heart monitor jump up and down on the other side of the room. She slumped down in the chair, brought her hand to her mouth, and promptly started to chew on the side of her thumb. Jake's dad, after at least an hour of intense conversation with a CIA agent who had calmed him down while divulging nothing, had just headed down to the cafeteria for some coffee. Gaia had actually turned down his offer to buy her food. The very idea of tasteless hospital grub made her lose her appetite. She'd been spending way too much time in hospitals lately.

"Gaia?"

She sat up straight and saw that Jake was rubbing his eyes with his fingertips. He blinked a few times and looked at her, confused. "Am I dead?"

Gaia laughed—a loud, relieved sort of bark. "No. You don't die from getting shot in the shoulder."

"The shoulder?"

He attempted to move his arm and winced and groaned. His head, which had come up about an inch off the pillow, flopped down again.

"Why does my head feel like someone ripped it in half?" he asked, his face crinkling up in pain.

"Concussion. You should probably just stay down,"

Gaia said. She got up and quickly flicked the light switch off so that the glare wouldn't cause him more pain. "You were knocked out when you fell," she explained, returning to her chair.

Jake managed a wry laugh and closed his eyes. "That's graceful." He took a deep breath and let it out slowly, gradually relaxing the muscles of his face. Gaia watched him, her heart pounding. There was something she wanted to say to him, but she was, as always, having trouble with the words.

A few more of his calming breaths and his eyes opened again. They were cool and clear now in the semidarkness—the only light in the room seeped in from the hallway.

"How's your leg?" he asked.

"It's fine," she replied. "Like I said. . . just a scratch."

"Great. You get a scratch, and I get an arm that feels like a sack of flour," Jake said with another laugh.

Gaia reddened and looked down at her hands in her lap. "Yeah. . . about that," she said, picking at her nonnails. "I wanted to. . . you know. . . thank you." He said nothing, and she finally forced herself to lift her chin—to look him in the eye. "You saved my life."

"Eh," Jake said, blowing it off. But he smiled nonetheless.

"Really. I was stupid. I should have known she wouldn't let it go," Gaia said. "So thanks."

"Don't thank me yet. You're going to be carrying

my books for the next few weeks," Jake shot back with a smirk.

Gaia smiled and looked down again, unsure of what to say next. Her legs were itching to run. She'd done what she'd come here to do, and now she was free to flee the hospital. But something made her stay right where she was. She didn't want to leave Jake alone. If she were honest with herself, she would have to admit that she didn't want to leave him, period.

There was this new but unmistakable pull between her and Jake. If she could, she would have made sure he was with her wherever she went. Having him around made her feel. . . safe. . . calm. . . almost normal.

"Gaia. . . how did you know?" Jake asked slowly.

"Know what?" Gaia asked, her face reddening as if he could hear her thoughts.

"That Tatiana was going to have those guys there?" Jake asked. "I mean, when I told you that the meeting was for the two of you and not the two of us, you knew right away that she was setting you up for something."

"I just know her," Gaia replied, realizing he'd want more than that. "Why did you tell me she asked you to bring me there? I'm sure she wanted it to be a surprise," she added with a touch of sarcasm.

"I didn't trust her," Jake replied. "When it came down to the two of you, I just. . . I knew she was in trouble, but somehow I knew I had to believe you."

Gaia's whole body warmed, and she looked away again. For all of Tatiana's flirting and damsel-in-distress routines, Jake had still seen who she really was. Gaia knew there was something great about this guy.

"Thanks," Gaia said.

"Look, I don't want to. . . you know. . . stick my nose in or whatever," Jake said. "But those guys tonight were pretty serious. I wasn't expecting. . ."

Gaia swallowed hard. "To get shot," she said, fresh guilt welling up inside her. "I never meant for you to—"

"No. I don't care about that. I'll be fine," Jake said. He looked her in the eye, and Gaia could tell there were a million questions he wanted to ask. She just wasn't sure if she could answer them. "I just. . . want to know if you're. . . if you're going to be okay."

A smile pulled at Gaia's lips. *That* was the most important thing on his mind? "I will be," she said. "Now that Tatiana is in custody. . . I'll be fine."

"Good," Jake said. He leaned back and looked at the ceiling. "God! She lied to me. Right to my face. All those fake, freakin' tears. She's insane."

"Pretty much," Gaia replied.

"So. . . you said she's in custody?" Jake asked, using his good arm to push himself up into a half-seated position. He let out a little groan as he settled back in.

Gaia took a deep breath and nodded. "She's been turned over to the proper authorities," she said.

Jake simply stared at her for a moment. "You ever gonna tell me what that means?" he asked, raising his eyebrows.

For a moment Gaia sat in silence, listening to the beeping heart monitor and the sounds of nurses and visitors walking past the room. She thought of all the secrets she'd kept over the last year, all the people she'd lost, all the people she'd tried to protect to no avail. She thought of Jake's open, honest face, of that afternoon when he'd readily offered to bring his friends to the dojo to help, of the way he'd looked at her as he threw himself in the path of the bullet that was meant for her heart.

He cared about her. He wanted her to be safe. He wanted to be at her side.

Maybe it was time for a change in her life. Maybe it was time to stop protecting and let someone protect her. Let someone in. Let someone be a true friend.

And so she looked at Jake, smiled, and meant it when she said, "I will. . . someday."

THE HANDCUFFS WERE LIKE ICE against Tatiana's bare wrists. The cold of the metal chair stung her skin, even through her clothes, and she felt like she was being refrigerated from the inside out. Even her bones were shivering. Her head slumped forward, pulling the muscles in her arms, which were secured behind her back. She sniffled, trying to keep her nose from running. Trying to keep that one sign of weakness at bay.

I've failed, she thought, staring down at the blood spatters on the thigh of her jeans. *I've failed you, Mother. I've failed myself.*

She sat in the center of a dim, gray, cinder-block-walled room. A two-way mirror hung on the far wall; a single lightbulb swung overhead. The only two pieces of furniture aside from her own chair were a wooden table and a high stool that stood next to the leaden door. Tatiana had no idea where she was, but she'd never felt so alone.

I'm worthless. I hope they just let me die in here, Tatiana thought, feeling her bruises throb, the cut across her left cheek sting. She'd gotten that just after the gun went off—just after Jake had slumped to the floor—dead, for all she knew. Not that she cared about him. He'd betrayed her. He'd ambushed her. He was a traitor.

Gaia had launched herself over his prone body and landed a backhand across Tatiana's face that had exploded behind her eye and knocked her out for a few moments. Long enough for Gaia and the Karate Squad to tie her up. Long enough for Ms. Moore to call in the CIA.

If I ever see her again, I'm going to kill her, Tatiana thought. *Next time I'll get it right.*

A loud clang echoed through the room as the lock on the heavy door slid free. Suddenly alert, Tatiana snapped up her head. The interrogation was about to begin. She could not be weak in the face of her enemy. She knew they'd probably hit her with the good-cop, bad-cop routine. It was standard procedure. She waited for the appearance of a couple of suited CIA agents, ready and more than willing to break her. Tatiana would not be broken.

The door swung open slowly, and Tatiana's brain almost exploded at the sight before her eyes. Gaia Moore—hair slicked back into a neat ponytail, a clean black sweater over a clean pair of jeans, and her standard black boots. No sign of a fight anywhere on her perfect little face. She stepped into the room, her eyes locked on Tatiana's, and the door swung shut behind her.

Somehow Tatiana managed to stare right back at Gaia. Stare through the confusion, the shame, the pain, the anger, the hatred. Her blood boiled and raced and melted away the cold. She refused to be the first to look away.

Gaia turned and picked up the stool by the wall. She set it down about two feet from Tatiana and perched herself on top of it. Now Tatiana saw the benefit of the higher stool. Gaia could look down on her— she could feel taller and more imposing. Tatiana lifted her chin and met her eyes. She was not intimidated.

"I'm here to tell you that the CIA has decided to give

you a choice," Gaia said slowly, deliberately. Tatiana seethed at her superior tone but refused to let slip the mask of bored defiance on her face. "If you tell me where my father is, they will let you join your mother in confinement," Gaia continued. "If you don't tell me, they're going to throw you in solitary."

Tatiana's eyes burned with instant tears. Her mother. She would get to be with her mother. She longed with every inch of her being to see Natasha again. It was all that mattered. It was all she had left. She ducked her chin so that Gaia wouldn't be looking right into her eyes when the first tear fell.

"Think about it, Tatiana," Gaia continued. "Solitary means a room smaller than this one—darker than this one. All alone. For as long as you decide to remain silent."

Oh God, I can't do this, Tatiana thought, her mind racing as she stared at the floor. *What if I tell them everything and go to my mother and she turns her back on me? She'll know I failed. I could never handle that.*

But she also wouldn't be able to handle solitary. She'd hardly been able to handle being alone for the last few days. She'd go crazy if they locked her up by herself. She'd go mad.

"Well?" Gaia said. "What do you say?"

Tatiana looked up at her, vision blurred, the words on the very tip of her tongue. All she had to do was say it and she'd be in her mother's arms again. All she had to do was talk.

But then she saw the shame and disappointment that would be in her mother's eyes. She saw her mother turning away as she ran to her. And the pain of that simple image was excruciating.

Tatiana turned her profile to Gaia and squeezed her eyes shut. She wouldn't tell. Not now. Not yet. She had to think. And right now she was too tired, too confused. She needed some time to process everything.

"Fine," Gaia spat, shoving the stool away from her. "You have twenty-four hours to make your decision."

The door swung open again as Gaia approached it, and Tatiana felt her glare at her one last time. Then she stepped out, and the door swung shut behind her. The resounding clang sounded with the finality of death. Finally Tatiana tipped her head forward and gave way to silent tears.

THE MOMENT GAIA WALKED INTO **Hyperawake** the fourth-floor office at the brownstone, Oliver turned away from his computer and looked at her with a never-before-seen excitement in his light eyes. Against her will, Gaia's heart leapt crazily. Even after everything she'd been through that day—the good-bye with Ed, the fight, the hospital, the one-on-one with Tatiana, she was suddenly hyperawake.

"What is it?" she asked, dropping her stuff on the floor and crossing the room. She stood at his side and squeezed her arms over her chest. "What's going on?"

"We've got him," Oliver said, smiling up at her. "We've found your father."

Inside, Gaia jumped up and down. . . she yelped and hugged Oliver, tackling him to the ground. . . she did cartwheels and somersaults and danced a jig worthy of *Riverdance.* Outside, she remained the picture of intense concentration.

"Where?" she asked.

"He's in Siberia. . . in a hospital there," Oliver said, sliding a few sheets of paper out of a large manila envelope. He handed over a glossy black-and-white photo of her father in a hospital bed, either sleeping or unconscious. His face was covered with a few days' beard. As expected, he did look exactly like Oliver had when she'd first seen him in the hospital. Lying on top of the blanket that covered his legs was a copy of a Russian newspaper, the date as clear as day in the top-right corner. The picture had been taken two days ago.

Gaia felt her mouth go dry as her eyes traveled to the medical monitors to the right of her father's bed. They were alight with lines and squiggles and numbers. Her father was alive. Or was two days ago.

"Thank you," Gaia said under her breath. "You found him. . . . Thank you."

Oliver smiled slightly and handed over another sheet of paper. "This is the address of the hospital," he said. "You'll have to fly to Minsk."

"Great," Gaia said, turning for the door. "I'm gone."

"No!"

Oliver stood up from his chair, scraping it back so fast, it fell over and clattered to the floor. Gaia stopped short and closed her eyes. Nothing was going to keep her from leaving right this very second. How could he even suggest otherwise?

"Gaia, the second you book that ticket, there are going to be hundreds of agents on your tail," Oliver said, each of his words hitting her back like tiny daggers. "I promise you, you will never make it to Russia alive. Never."

"Well, then what am I supposed to do?" Gaia demanded, whirling around again, clutching the papers and the photograph in her hands. "Why give me this information if you expect me to do nothing?"

Oliver stepped over to her, reached out, and placed his hands on her shoulders. "I expect you to wait," he said, eliciting an eye roll and a sigh from Gaia. "Just two days. In two days I can get you a legitimate passport with a new name for you to travel under. I can have a whole history made up for the new you in case anyone decides to check."

He squeezed her shoulders, and Gaia looked down. She knew that he was right—that this was the only logical way to do things. But how could she? How could she wait two whole days?

"And I can have the same thing done for myself," Oliver continued.

Gaia raised her chin and looked into his eyes, her pulse thumping in her ears—her heart a tangled mess of conflicting emotions. Had he really just said what she thought he'd said?

"I'm coming with you," he added firmly. "You're not going anywhere alone. Not anymore."

Two days.

Forty-eight hours.

Two thousand, eight hundred and eighty minutes.

One hundred seventy-two thousand, eight hundred seconds.

And I'll be on my way to find my father. And this time I'm bringing him home. For good.

here is a
sneak peek of
Fearless™ #29:

LUST

I guess the only time most people think about blood is when it's gushing out of their veins and they need to find a Band-Aid—or an emergency room—to keep it from messing up the white carpet. But I'm thinking about it a lot lately. Little red platelets and big white corpuscles rushing through everyone's veins. Keeping us alive as long as it stays on its dark little course—but signaling weakness or death when it wanders off the path, out into the light, to spill on the ground.

Funny thing about blood—it also connects people. There it is, hidden inside your skin, yet it manages to call out to other blood, related blood, inside someone else's skin. You might have nothing else in common, but that red stuff really is thicker than water. There's nobody in the world I should have more cause to hate than Oliver. Or should I say, Loki. He has engineered more destruction—starting with my own mother, the

woman who created my own blood—than
anyone else in my life. So a bout
of postcoma confusion has forced
his pre-Loki, kinder and gentler
Oliver personality to emerge, and
suddenly he regrets his evil ways.

At best, I should feel indif-
ferent toward him. But because we
share blood, I find myself drawn
to him. I find myself willing to
try to trust him—this new,
remorseful Oliver—because our DNA
matches up so nicely.

Am I just a sucker? A girl so
lonely she'll cling to any sem-
blance of a family connection? Or
is this an instinct, speaking
through the layers of primordial
history, telling me the tide has
turned for Oliver?

Let's hope it's the latter.

Let's hope it's the blood
that's letting me forgive him.
Anyone else would get nothing from
me but my everlasting hate. Like
Natasha and Tatiana. The mother-
daughter team from the third ring
of hell. A couple of lying, con-
niving females who took my dad

from me and almost had me con-
vinced he was dead. But he can't
be dead. My blood would tell me if
he was. They're still going to
pay, though. Maybe with their own
blood. If I get half a chance, you
can bet that'll be the case.

But that's so not a priority.
What's important now—what's got
to happen before anything else—is
I've got to find my dad. My real
blood link. Even closer to me
than Oliver. He's the one I owe
my loyalty to. And I'm going to
find him. Come hell or high
water, the blood pumping in my
veins is going to give me the
strength to reach around the
globe and find him. You can bet
on that.

She had to

remember

to keep her

distance

unfamiliar

this

terrain

time—

within her

heart and

out in the

world.

Dangerously Accurate

GAIA SAT SLUMPED IN AN UNFORGIV-ing wood-and-metal chair as she cycled through the seven local stations one more time, looking for something that would amuse her and Jake in his hospital room. The television, which looked about twenty years old, was bolted to the ceiling and made a disconcerting fuzzy noise whenever a channel was changed, like the *cchk* sound at the beginning and end of a walkie-talkie broadcast. The static was only marginally less interesting than daytime TV.

"Is this *Judge Judy*?" Gaia wanted to know.

"No, that's a different show," Jake said, pointing to the screen. "It looks like a judge show, but then they bring in therapists and it turns into a corny lovefest where everybody's hugging and crying, even though tomorrow they're going to go back to throwing chairs at each other."

"You need better health insurance. This no-cable thing is a problem."

"Aren't you supposed to be in school?" Jake asked again. Gaia glared at him. Forcing herself to ignore the way his black hair fell on his forehead just right, even after a full twenty-four hours of lying in a hospital bed. And the way his green eyes sparkled as he asked the

5

question he knew would annoy her. And the muscles she could see even through the loose hospital gown he wore. If he got out of bed, she'd get a prime view of his butt. She forced herself to ignore that, too.

"Didn't I already sidestep that question?" she wanted to know.

"Yeah, that's why I have to ask it again. I'm in a weakened state. I'd think you'd be more considerate—it's tiring, all this verbal tangoing, you know."

"Whatever. I skipped again," she admitted. "I can't sit around in school. I'm too agitated."

"What? Because of this?" Jake shrugged. Gaia tried not to think about the fact that he'd been shot when he'd been ambushed along with her. *Because* of her. So what if it turned out to be nothing more than a flesh wound? He was hurt because he'd gotten in the way of people who were after Gaia. And that made her feel ill.

He wasn't the first person to end up lying on a metal cot with a tube in his arm because of her. And she felt a leaden certainty that he wouldn't be the last.

"No, not because of that," she said sheepishly, glancing at the bandages enveloping his powerful shoulder. "You know why."

"Because you're worried about those visas," he said, taking the remote from her hand and switching the TV off. "You're going to make yourself crazy, you know."

"Oh, I'm already there, so there's nothing to worry about," she told him.

"Yeah, but. . . I mean, you have to wait a couple days anyway, right? Why can't you just go to school and avoid getting in trouble?"

Gaia blinked at him. "What are you, a boy scout?" she asked.

Jake laughed. "No, I'm just saying you could pass the time at school as easily as you can pass it sitting here."

Gaia knew he was right. She didn't know why she had such an aversion to school. Maybe it was because she already knew everything that was being droned about at the front of the classroom. Her dad—her dad and her mom, actually—had made sure of that, making her take advantage of her sharp intellect from the moment she could read. Maybe she just hated being fenced in. Maybe she was worried that another strike would hurt the students around her. Or maybe she just wanted to be here, at the hospital, with Jake.

"Oh, why start behaving now," she mustered. "It would just confuse everyone."

"You know what I think?" Jake gave her a sidelong look.

"No, in fact, I don't possess that particular skill," Gaia responded dryly.

"I think you like the drama," he said with a tiny nod. "You like getting the principal all pissed off at you and driving your teachers up the wall. Because you know you can pull a passing grade out of your ass, and you like the challenge."

"Oh, really. Is that what you think?"

"Yeah. Plus, now that I know how crazy your life has been, it makes even more sense. You'd hate to feel settled and centered in any part of your life, wouldn't you? That would just be too unfamiliar to stand." Jake was enjoying this, Gaia could see that. She was acting nonchalant, but inside she was squirming with discomfort under the probing spotlight of this much attention. Not to mention that his theory sounded dangerously accurate.

"Hey, I have a great idea, Jake. Why don't you get out of my head and back into your hospital bed? I think it's time for your lower G.I. series."

"Oh, hoooo!" Jake laughed at the sharp tone in Gaia's voice. "Man, are you easy to tease!"

"You're annoying," Gaia told him. "I'm going to request a male nurse for your next sponge bath."

Just then the door clunked open and Jake's father entered the room, along with a stout old woman. Gaia stood up as if she'd been caught pulling the wings off a fly. Mr. Montone didn't know why Jake had been ambushed—they couldn't know for sure that it was Gaia's fault—but Gaia was sure he'd still be angry at her. Surely he'd figure it couldn't be a coincidence that the first time his golden boy had gotten shot, it had been when he was with his mysterious new friend.

"Gaia!" Mr. Montone came straight for her and gave her a... hug? Gaia's nerve endings did a little confused dance—they'd been expecting a slap, or at least the cold shoulder.

"Thank you for getting Jake to the hospital," Mr. Montone said. "When I heard he was with you, I was so glad—that he had a friend so close, I mean. Ma, this is Jake's friend Gaia. The one who got him to the hospital."

"You do so good!" the old woman said, reaching up to grab Gaia by the cheeks and give her an affectionate—and powerful—squeeze.

"A lot of girls your age are somewhat—flighty," Mr. Montone added. "Might have panicked and run home."

"Oh no," Gaia stammered. "I mean, I didn't really—" *Shut up and quit while you're ahead*, she muttered internally. *For once someone thinks you did something right. You'd better enjoy it.*

"Dad, Nonna, what are you guys doing here?" Jake asked. "Is something wrong?"

The door opened again. A nervous-looking young doctor in a white coat shuffled in, looking like he'd rather be dealing with an obstructed bowel.

"Excuse me. I understand you want to take Jake home?" he asked, with all the authority of a kid who'd missed his curfew.

"How to put this nicely?" Jake's grandmother said. "It's not so much that we *want* to take him home. We *gonna* take him home."

The doctor looked to Jake's dad for help, but he

just shrugged and started packing Jake's things into a duffel bag.

"Mrs. Montone, I really must tell you, we'd prefer it if we could watch Jake for one more night."

"Watch him what, starve to death because of your hospital food? I need to get some braciola into him before he fades to nothing."

"We'd just like to observe. . . Oh, fine," the doctor said resignedly.

"Good man," Mr. Montone said, patting him on the back. "Don't worry, I can watch him. I know what to look for—infection, gangrene. I work at Mount Sinai, you know."

"Yes, sir."

It was amazing. Mr. Montone looked like an older Jake, but with salt-and-pepper hair, a bit of a belly, and in corduroys and a tweed jacket. He peered at Jake over his half-glasses and said, "You. Up."

"Gaia, do you mind?" Jake asked.

"What? Oh!" Gaia got flustered. "I'll wait in the hall." She caught a glimpse of him sitting up and shifting over in bed and thought of his butt again.

Quit that, she thought, shutting the door behind her. Immediately she realized she should have just made her excuses and left. Of course, she could still just leave, but she hadn't said good-bye, and Jake's family would think she was weird. But if she barged back in now, she might catch him in a compromised state, and that would be too embarrassing for words.

And why do you care what Jake's family thinks? she asked herself.

I don't, she answered. *Who cares? Just because his father fed me the best homemade dinner I've had since I was a kid and welcomed me into his home. And just because his son is basically my only friend. I don't give a hoot what they think of me.* But still she stood in the hallway, shifting her weight from one foot to the other with nervous energy, until they came back out.

Jake was fully clothed, except that he hadn't managed to get a T-shirt over his bandages, so his loose flannel button-down shirt fell open at the chest. His father and grandmother followed behind him, arguing over which one should carry the duffel bag.

"Gimme that. You've got the bad back," his grandmother ordered.

"I've got it. It's not heavy," his dad said.

"Not heavy till you're in bed and need a heat-wrap. Come on, give."

Jake slowed down so they had to pass him, then let the elevator door close without him.

"See you downstairs," he called out as his grandmother tried to hit the door-open button and failed. "The hospital would have been some welcome peace and quiet," he said to Gaia, grinning.

"I think they're great," she said.

"They are. But Nonna's a bit much." He sighed and hit the down button so they could get on the next elevator.

"Are you sure you should be going home?" Gaia asked.

"Oh, yeah," Jake said. "I fully expected my dad to show up and yank me out of here. He always says the best way to get sicker is to spend time in a hospital. I guess from working in them. This thing does ache, though."

"Yeek." Gaia peered at the big bandage. "I don't think you're going to be doing much intramural karate."

Jake groaned. "I know," he lamented. "You're off the hook, though. If I'm not competing, we won't win, anyway."

"God, you've got the fattest head!" Gaia complained. "You think I couldn't beat everyone single-handedly?"

"You could, but you won't," he pointed out. "I was really looking forward to it, though. I was all revved up for the competition. Without it, the next few weeks are going to be so boring. And I'm going to get so out of shape."

Gaia felt the bud of an idea fatten in her head. "Hmm," she said.

"Hmm, what?" Jake asked, poking the button a few more times.

"Hmm, I was just thinking. When I was going through my martial-arts training, my dad showed me a bunch of techniques for working out that give various muscle groups a rest. I could teach them to you,

12

just so your precious muscle mass doesn't evaporate during your recovery."

"Gaia Moore, are you offering to be my personal trainer?"

She rolled her eyes. "Yeah, right. If you're going to be an idiot about it, I won't bother."

Jake smacked her lightly in the back of the head. "Cut it out," he said. "I'm sorry. I would be really grateful if you could show me your special commando workout."

"Fine. I will," Gaia said.

"But only if you go to school tomorrow."

"Ugh. Fine."

"Of course, you're going to be gone within a day or two," Jake pointed out, as the elevator finally arrived and the doors creaked open. "Your visa's going to come through and you're going to be out of here, and I'll be left with atrophying muscles and a gunshot wound."

For a moment, Gaia had a vision of Sam Moon's scarred back—another wounded friend, a love destroyed by the life she was forced to lead. She had to remember to keep her distance this time. Within her heart, and out in the world. She wouldn't let that happen to Jake.

"Oh, that visa's never going to come," she said, refusing to betray the emotions roiling inside her gut. "You'll be sick of me and my commando workout."

She was silent, watching the numbers light up in

13

descending order. This was the slowest elevator in the world. She noticed Jake giving her a look.

"What?" she snapped.

"I think it's funny," he said.

"What's funny?"

"The way every single thought in your head goes walking across your face before you shove it back in its closet," Jake said. "You really think that because you don't say things out loud, you can deny they're there, don't you?"

"All right, smart guy. So what thoughts am I repressing?" she asked, crossing her arms and still staring as 9 flipped to 8 with agonizing sluggishness.

"Oh, no. I'm not making things easier for you. You'll open your mouth when you're good and ready, not before."

Gaia clamped her mouth tightly closed, sucking her lips in for extra emphasis and refusing to look at Jake. He was so close to her, she could feel the heat from his body making the left side of her face flush. Without her meaning to, her eyes flicked toward him, then away again. The expression in his eyes—he seemed to *know* her in a way that others didn't. Gaia wasn't sure whether that was good or bad. He was teasing her, daring her to feel something for him. It was maddening, annoying.

The doors finally opened. "Jake!" Mrs. Montone called out, her arms extended as if she were about to reach in and yank him out. "Why you sneak off like that? Come here."

Jake shot Gaia one last look and joined his father

and grandmother, who draped a coat carefully over his shoulders.

"Gaia, can you get home all right?" Mr. Montone asked. "Should we drop you somewhere? We've got a car service waiting."

"Oh no, it's all right," Gaia promised. "I can take the subway."

"Are you sure? It's no trouble."

Gaia was touched. If he'd had any idea of what she'd been through in her life, he'd know that a midday subway was hardly an inconvenience to her.

"I promise. It was nice to see you again. And nice to meet you, Mrs. Montone."

"Yeah, I see you again," she said, nodding cheerfully.

"So I'll see you tomorrow after school?" Jake asked. "You'll show me that stuff we were talking about?"

Gaia felt herself nod. Maddening, yes. Annoying, yes. But whether it was out of guilt or some kind of fascination, Jake was now an official friend of Gaia Moore.

OLIVER SEARCHED THROUGH THE

Subconscious Voice

databases he had found stored on his computer for half a day, just to gain access to his own information. It was like he was trying to put together one of those all-black jigsaw puzzles—in the dark, during a windstorm. If something looked familiar, he then had to ask himself why, and what it might connect to, and how he should approach it. He felt like a blind man in a maelstrom.

Uncovering this information required the highest level of mental functioning. It was exhausting for someone who had just woken out of a coma. But that wasn't the hard part. The hard part was that to access some of the memories he needed—passwords, log-in names, locations of files, meanings of notes—he had to force some of Loki's memories to the surface. And Oliver was not a computer. He couldn't just pull up one file out of a folder and leave the rest safely closed. As he exposed one memory to the light, others tried to bubble up as well. And it took all his psychic energy to keep those memories submerged.

He was dancing a dangerous tango with his evil former self.

He took a long drink of bottled water and turned his eyes to the screen again. He had to secure transportation for himself and Gaia. Airline tickets. How did this work again? He had to get the passports in another name, the visas to match, enough tickets for everyone. . . The screen began to swim in front of him. It seemed to morph into a television screen. On it, he saw a man—a man dressed as a doctor—in an antiseptic room; a white room, but not a hospital. A loft of some kind. A young woman was there—a girl, a friend of Gaia's. Something in him told him that. The scene was new but dripping with familiarity, like the subconscious voice in dreams that acts as narrator for unfamiliar terrain.

The girl bent over and the doctor injected her with something. Oliver squinted to see more clearly. Then the screen split; on one side, he saw the beautiful woman struck blind as a result of the injection. On the other side, he saw the doctor raise his face. With horror, Oliver recognized the eyes staring back at him from the television screen. They were his own.

Jolted, he jumped back, knocking his chair to the floor with a clatter. The noise made him look down, and when he looked back, the taunting television screen had become his computer again—his safe, familiar computer, quietly listing his old contacts for him to pore over.

"Loki," he said out loud. "It was Loki, and I have control over him."

He straightened the chair and placed it in front of his desk again, glancing nervously at the computer screen. But it was still covered in calm, static numbers. No more streaming video straight from his buried internal hard drive. Oliver took a deep breath and sat down again.

He needed to find a few contacts who would still do favors for him. He needed to check those favors, to be sure he was not being scammed. He had to secure passports and visas. His brother's life depended on it. Gaia's happiness depended on it.

He mustered his energy and forced himself back to work.

SIMON PULSE FICTION

Edgy, Daring, Real

Available now:

Coming soon:

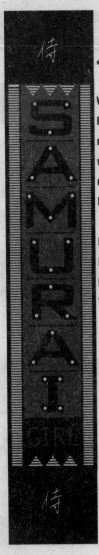

When I was six months old, I dropped from the sky—the lone survivor of a deadly Japanese plane crash. The newspapers named me Heaven. I was adopted by a wealthy family in Tokyo, pampered, and protected. For nineteen years, I thought I was lucky.

I'm learning how wrong I was.

I've lost the person I love most.
I've begun to uncover the truth about my family.
Now I'm being hunted. I must fight back, or die.
The old Heaven is gone.

I AM SAMURAI GIRL.

A new series from Simon Pulse

The Book of the Sword
The Book of the Shadow

BY CARRIE ASAI

Available in bookstores now